"Honestly, Rick. I Was Going To Tell You About The Girls When You Came Home. I Want Them To Know Their Daddy."

Shaking his head, he grabbed her upper arms, pulling her close.

Sadie felt heat radiating off his body and reaching into hers. Just the touch of his hands on her skin was enough to start small brushfires in her blood.

His gaze moved over her features like a slow caress. And his eyes were still churning with too many emotions to count. "I want to believe you, Sadie."

She tipped her head back to meet his eyes. "You can trust me, Rick."

"That's to be seen. But there's only one thing to be done now."

A ripple of apprehension scuttled through Sadie and still she asked, "What's that?"

"We're getting married."

Dear Reader,

Being invited to be a part of a continuity series for Harlequin is always an honor. But I have to say, I was especially excited to write one of the Texas Cattleman's Club books. I love this series myself, so writing one was a treat!

In *One Night, Two Heirs,* you'll meet Sadie Price and Rick Pruitt. They both grew up in Royal, Texas, but never really connected. Rick was raised on the family ranch when his career military father wasn't dragging them all around the world. Sadie was raised to be the perfect daughter—never a step out of line. Until of course, one spectacular night that changed both of them forever.

But it's not just Sadie and Rick's relationship going through some major upheavals! There are all kinds of interesting things happening in Royal. Big changes are floating around the TCC and not everyone is happy about that!

I really hope you enjoy Rick and Sadie's story. I had such a good time writing it—I can't wait to see what you think of it.

Visit my website at www.maureenchild.com and take a second to email me. I love to hear from my readers.

Happy Reading!

Maureen

MAUREEN CHILD

ONE NIGHT, TWO HEIRS

Harlequin®

Desire

Special thanks and acknowledgment to Maureen Child for her contribution to the Texas Cattleman's Club: The Showdown miniseries.

Recycling programs
for this product may
not exist in your area.

ISBN-13: 978-0-373-73109-1

ONE NIGHT, TWO HEIRS

www.Harlequin.com

Printed in U.S.A.

Books by Maureen Child

Silhouette Desire

†*Scorned by the Boss* #1816
†*Seduced by the Rich Man* #1820
†*Captured by the Billionaire* #1826
††*Bargaining for King's Baby* #1857
††*Marrying for King's Millions* #1862
††*Falling for King's Fortune* #1868
High-Society Secret Pregnancy #1879
Baby Bonanza #1893
An Officer and a Millionaire #1915
Seduced Into a Paper Marriage #1946
††*Conquering King's Heart* #1965
††*Claiming King's Baby* #1971
††*Wedding at King's Convenience* #1978
††*The Last Lone Wolf* #2011
Claiming Her Billion-Dollar Birthright #2024
††*Cinderella & the CEO* #2043
Under the Millionaire's Mistletoe #2056
  "The Wrong Brother"
Have Baby, Need Billionaire #2059

Harlequin Desire

††*King's Million-Dollar Secret* #2083
One Night, Two Heirs #2096

†Reasons for Revenge
††Kings of California

MAUREEN CHILD

is a California native who loves to travel. Every chance they get, she and her husband are taking off on another research trip. The author of more than sixty books, Maureen loves a happy ending and still swears that she has the best job in the world. She lives in Southern California with her husband, two children and a golden retriever with delusions of grandeur. Visit Maureen's website at www.maureenchild.com.

To Charles Griemsman, a world-class editor.
Thanks for making working on this continuity
such a pleasure, Charles!

* * *

Don't miss a single book in this series!

Texas Cattleman's Club: The Showdown
*They are rich and powerful, hot and wild.
For these Texans, it's showdown time!*

One

Marine First Sergeant Rick Pruitt had thirty days' leave to decide the rest of his life.

"But no pressure," he muttered and loped across Main Street. He lifted a hand to wave at Joe Davis. His boyhood buddy was still driving that battered, dusty red truck. Rick paused on the sidewalk when his friend pulled to the curb to talk to him. Joe rolled the passenger-side window down and grinned. "Look what the east Texas wind blew home. When'd you get here, Rick?"

"Yesterday." Rick tipped the brim of his hat back a bit, leaned his forearms on the window frame and only winced a little at the red-hot feel of the metal against his arms. If there was one thing a Texas boy learned to deal with at an early age, it was the summer heat.

Right now, the sun was blazing down from a brassy sky and there wasn't so much as a hint of a cloud in sight. July in Texas was good training, weather wise, for a marine who spent his time deployed to the Middle East.

"You home to stay?" Joe asked.

"That's a good question," Rick replied.

"And not much of an answer."

Truth was, Rick didn't have an answer yet. He had spent a lot of years in the Corps and he had enjoyed them all. He loved serving his country. He was damn proud to wear the uniform of a U.S. Marine. But, he thought, glancing at his surroundings, he'd missed a hell of a lot, too. He hadn't been here when either of his parents died. Hadn't been around to run the family ranch, instead trusting in their longtime foreman to do the heavy lifting. And, since the Pruitt ranch was one of the biggest in Texas, that was some serious duty to push off on someone else.

Funny, all those years in the Corps and not one of his buddies had ever known that he was one of the richest men in Texas. He had always been just another marine—and that's how he had wanted it.

He'd been around the world and back. Had seen more, done more than most men ever would. But, he thought, his heart had always been here. In Royal.

Rick smiled and shrugged. "It's the only answer I've got. For right now, I've got thirty days' leave and decisions to make."

"Well," Joe told him, "if you want any help deciding, you give me a call."

"I will." Rick looked at his old friend. They'd grown up together, had their first beers—and hangovers—together. They'd played side by side on the high school football team. Joe had stayed put in Royal, married Tina, his high school sweetheart, had two kids now and was in charge of the family garage. Rick had gone to college, joined the Corps and had come close to love only once.

For a second or two, he allowed himself to remember the girl he'd once thought unattainable. The woman whose memory had kept him going through some ugly days in the last few years. There were some women, he figured, just designed to get into a man's soul. And this one surely had.

"While you're in town, we should do some fishing," Joe said, drawing Rick up out of his thoughts.

Grateful, he said, "Sounds like a plan. You get Tina to make us some of her famous fried chicken for lunch and we'll make a day of it at the ranch lake."

"That's a deal." Joe stretched out his right hand. "It really is good to see you home, Rick. And if you want my opinion, maybe it's time you stayed home."

"Thanks, Joe." Rick shook his friend's hand and blew out a breath. "It's good to be back."

Nodding, Joe said, "I've got to get back to the shop. Mrs. Donley's old sedan had another breakdown and that woman hasn't let up on me for days about it."

Rick actually shivered. Mrs. Marianne Donley, the high school math teacher, could bring a cold chill to the spine of anybody in Royal who had survived her geometry class.

Joe saw the shudder and nodded grimly. "Exactly. I'll call you about the fishing."

"Do that." Rick slapped his hands against the truck, then stepped back as Joe pulled away.

He stood there for a long minute, just soaking up the feeling of being home again. Only three days ago, he'd been with his men in the middle of a firefight. Today, he was on a street corner of a quiet little town, watching traffic roll by.

And he wasn't sure which of those two places he most belonged.

Rick had always wanted to be a marine. And the truth was, since his parents were both gone now, there wasn't much to hold him in Royal. Yeah, there was the duty he felt to the Pruitt dynasty. The ranch had been in the family for more than a hundred and fifty years. But there were caretakers out there, a foreman and his wife, the housekeeper who lived in and saw to it that the Pruitt ranch went on without him. Just as Royal had.

He narrowed his gaze to cut the glare of the summer sun and quickly scanned his surroundings. Things didn't change in small-town America, he told himself and was inwardly glad of it. He liked knowing that he could go away for a couple years and come home to find the place just as he'd left it.

The only thing that had changed, he admitted silently, was him.

Tugging the brim of his Stetson lower over his eyes, Rick shook his head and turned back toward the Texas Cattleman's Club. If there was one place for a man to go to catch up on the news about town, it was the TCC. Besides, he was looking forward to the cool quiet. The chance to do a little thinking—not to mention the appeal of a cold glass of beer and a steak sandwich in the dining room.

"Bradford Price, you're living in the Stone Age." Sadie Price glared up at her older brother and wasn't the slightest bit surprised to notice he wasn't denying her accusation. In fact, he looked proud.

"If that's your roundabout way of telling me that I'm a man of tradition, then I'm all right with that." Brad leaned down and kept his voice low. "And I don't appreciate my baby sister coming in here to read me the riot act because I don't agree with her."

Sadie silently counted to ten. Then twenty. Then she gave up. Her temper wouldn't be cooled by counting, or the multiplication tables or even with thoughts of her twin daughters' smiling faces. She had been pushed too far and, like a true Price, she was fighting mad.

The main room of the Texas Cattleman's Club might not have been the perfect spot for a throw-down, she thought, but it was too late to back off now. Even if she had wanted to.

"I didn't move back to Royal from Houston just to sit at home and do nothing, Brad."

In fact, now that she was home again, she intended to make a name for herself. To get involved. And the TCC was just the place to make a start. She had been thinking about this all night and the fact that her older brother was making things hard on her wouldn't change her mind.

"Fine," he said, throwing both hands high. "Do something. Anything. Just not here."

"Women are a part of the club's world now, Brad," she insisted, glancing over at the two elderly men sitting in brown leather club chairs. At her quick look, they both lifted the newspapers they were hiding behind and pretended they hadn't been watching.

Typical, Sadie thought. The men in this once-exclusive club were determined to ignore progress of any kind. Heck, they'd had to be hog-tied to get them to allow women in the club at all. And they still weren't happy about it.

"You don't need to remind me of that," Brad said tightly. "Haven't I got Abigail Langley riding me like a bull in the rodeo? That woman's about to drive me out of my mind and I'm damned if I'm going to take it from you, too."

She hissed in a breath. "You are the most hardheaded, ornery…"

"I'm going to be in charge around here, little sister," he told her. "And you'd best remember that."

Here being the Texas Cattleman's Club, of course. Brad was planning on running for club president and if he won, Sadie knew darn well that the TCC would stay in the dark ages.

Sadie bit down on her bottom lip to keep the furious words that wanted to spill from her locked inside. Honestly, the TCC had been the bulwark of stubborn men for more than a hundred years.

Even the decor in the place reeked of testosterone. Paneled walls, dark brown leather furniture, hunting prints on the walls and a big-screen TV, the better to watch every single Texas sporting event. Until recently, women had only been allowed in the dining room or on the tennis courts. But now, thanks to Abby Langley being an honorary member—with full club privileges— due to her late husband Richard's name and history with the club, all of that was changing. And the women in Royal were counting on the fact that now that Pandora's box had been opened, the men in town wouldn't be able to close it again.

But if dealing with her brother was a sign of how difficult change was going to be, Sadie knew she and the other females in town were in for a whale of a fight.

"Look," she said, trying for her most reasonable tone—which wasn't easy when faced with a head as hard as her brother's—"the club is looking to build a new headquarters. I'm a landscape designer. I can help.

I've got the name of a great architect. And I did some sketches for the new grounds that—"

"Sadie…" Brad sighed and shook his head. "Nothing's been decided. We don't need an architect. Or a landscape designer. Or a damn interior decorator."

"You could at least listen to me," she argued.

"I may have to put up with Abby Langley giving me grief, but I don't have to listen to my baby sister," Brad said. "Now go on home, Sadie."

He walked away.

Just turned his back and walked off as if she didn't matter at all. Fuming silently, Sadie thought briefly about chasing him down and giving him another piece of her mind. But that would only give the old coots like Buck Johnson and Henry Tate even more to gossip about.

Her gaze shifted to those two men, still hiding behind their newspapers as if they were completely oblivious to what was going on. Well, Sadie knew better. Those two had heard every word of her argument with her brother and by tonight, she expected that they would have repeated it dozens of times. And men said *women* were gossips.

Grumbling under her breath, she tucked her cream-colored leather bag beneath her arm, got a hard grip on the folder of sketches she'd brought along with her and stormed for the front door. The sound of her needle-thin heels clicked against the wood floor like a frantic heartbeat.

Disappointment and anger warred inside her. She'd really hoped that she would be able to at least count on her brother's support. But she should have known better. Brad was like a throwback to an earlier generation. He liked his women to be pretty pieces of arm candy and he liked the club just as it was—a male bastion against the ever-encroaching idea of equality of the sexes.

"He's a caveman," Sadie muttered, rushing out of the dark interior of the club into the bright sunlight of a July morning in Texas.

She was still running on pure temper and her eyes were so dazzled by the brilliant light, she didn't see the man until she crashed right into him.

One day back in his hometown and Rick Pruitt ran smack into a tornado. A tall, sleek, blond tornado with eyes as blue as the Texas sky and legs that went on forever. He'd been thinking about her only a minute or two before and now here she was. She stormed out of the Texas Cattleman's Club in such a fury, she'd run right into him only to bounce off like a pebble skipping across the surface of a lake.

He reached out to grab her shoulders and steady her. Then she lifted those big blue eyes up to him and the look on her face said clearly that he was the last person on earth she had expected to see.

"Mornin', Sadie," he said softly, letting his gaze sweep over the patrician features he remembered so well. "If you're really looking to run me over, you should maybe try it in a car. You're not nearly big enough to do it on foot."

She blinked at him. Her face paled and her eyes were wide and shining with shock. "Rick? What are you doing here?"

A long, humming second or two passed between them and that was all it took to get Rick's blood rushing and his body tightening. But Sadie swayed unsteadily.

"Hey," he asked. "Are you okay?"

"Fine," she murmured, though she didn't look it. "I'm

just surprised to see you, that's all. I didn't know you were home."

"Only arrived yesterday," he told her. "Guess the town gossip chain needs a little time to get up and running."

"I suppose so."

Her cheeks got even paler and she looked uneasy. Rick wondered why.

She shook her head. "I'm sorry about running into you. Coming out of the gloom of that man-cave into the bright daylight, I couldn't see and I was just so darn mad at Brad...."

Good to know, he told himself. He'd much rather she be furious with her brother than him. The one night they'd spent together had been haunting him for three long years. He'd spent a lot of time in the desert, remembering her taste, her touch. She was the kind of woman who slipped up on a man. Got under his defenses. Which was why he'd been glad to be leaving for his tour of duty right after their night together. He hadn't been looking for permanent back then, and Sadie Price was not the kind of woman to settle for a one-night stand.

He took a breath, inhaling her scent—that soft swirl of summer rain and flowers that always seemed to cling to her skin. That scent had stayed with him while he was deployed. And it didn't seem to matter where he was stationed or the misery that surrounded him...if he closed his eyes, she was there.

Thoughts of her had pulled him through some dark times. Looking down into her blue eyes, he could only think, *Damn, it's good to be home.*

"How about you?" he asked. "Last I heard you were living in Houston." Which was why he'd planned to drive into the city to look her up in a day or two. Much handier this way—having her right here in Royal.

"I was," she said and chewed at her bottom lip. Her gaze shifted from him. "I, um, moved back a few weeks ago."

"You okay?" he asked, noticing just how nervous she really was. Shaken, really, and he didn't like how pale she was, either. In fact, she looked small and fragile and every protective instinct he had rose to the surface, temporarily, at least burying his physical reaction to her.

"You know what? Let's just go back inside and sit in the cool for a minute. You don't look too steady on your feet."

She shook her head and said, "Oh, I'm fine, really. I just…"

"You're not fine. You look like you're going to pass out. This heat'll kill you if you're not careful. Come on." He took her elbow in a firm grip and steered her right back into the clubhouse.

"Really, Rick. I don't need to rest, I just need to go home."

"And you can, as soon as you've cooled off a little." He drew her to the bench seat beneath the legendary plaque that read Leadership, Justice and Peace.

She took a breath and Rick watched her gather herself. Her fingers clutched at her purse until her knuckles whitened and he had to wonder what the hell had her so upset? Was it seeing him again? Was she embarrassed by the memory of their night together?

"What's going on, Sadie?" he whispered and shook his head as one of the club attendants stepped up to see if he could help.

She laughed shortly, but there was no humor in it. Her

gaze lifted to his and he read worry and trepidation in her eyes. Now he was really confused. "Just talk to me."

For most of his life, Sadie Price had been the dream girl for him. She was beautiful, popular and even as kids, out of his league. Rick ran with a crowd that didn't appreciate the country-club parties that Sadie and her friends attended. He'd always thought of her as pretty much perfect, except for the prim and proper attitude. He used to dream about getting past all of her barriers to find out who she really was.

Then he'd joined the Corps and Sadie married a rat bastard who'd ended up cheating on her and making her miserable. Three years ago though, Sadie had been divorced and Rick was about to ship out for Afghanistan when they ran into each other at Claire's restaurant. They'd shared a drink, then dinner…then a hell of a lot more.

Just remembering that night had his body stirring to life again with a kind of hunger he'd never known before. After three long years, she was close enough to touch again. And damned if he was going to waste any time.

"You're just as beautiful as I remember," he said, lifting one hand to smooth her silky blond hair back from her cheek. His fingertips skimmed along her skin and he felt a jolt of heat hit him hard.

She sucked in a breath of air at his touch and he smiled to know that she felt the same sizzle he had.

"You know, why don't we head over to Claire's?" He leaned in closer. "We could get some lunch and catch up. Tell me everything you've been up to the last few years."

"What I've been up to," she repeated, then huffed out

a sigh and looked up into his eyes. "That's going to take some time. Oh, God. Rick…we really have to talk."

"That's what I'm saying," he told her, a smile curving his mouth.

"No," she said, "I mean we have to *talk*." She looked around and seemed relieved that no one was close by before she turned back to him and added, "But not here."

"All right," he said, a little wary now. What the hell was going on with her? At first she'd just seemed shocked to see him. Now she was a little jumpy. Not exactly the welcome-home response he would have hoped for. "You want to tell me what this is all about?"

"Not really," she admitted.

"Sadie…"

She stood up, tucked her purse under her arm and said, "Just, take me to my parents' house, will you Rick? I'm staying with Dad until I get my own place. Once we're there, I'll explain everything."

Standing, he nodded. Whatever the hell was going on, Rick would deal with it as he did everything else in his life. Head-on. "Right. Then let's get going."

Two

Sitting in Rick Pruitt's black truck brought back a flood of memories. Three years ago, she and Rick had shared one amazingly hot, sexy night that had changed her life forever. The next morning he left, reporting for a tour of duty in the Middle East.

And maybe that was partly why Sadie had given into her impulse to grab at that one night with him. She had known he'd be leaving again right away. But the reality was, Sadie had just needed someone. Back then, she had felt as though she was disappearing. Becoming nothing more than the socialite daughter of a wealthy man. She never did anything for herself. Never stepped out of line from what was expected.

Until that night. Neither of them had made the other any promises. Neither of them had been looking for anything more than exactly what they had found together. A little magic.

But the truth was, that night with Rick had changed Sadie's life forever—and he had no idea.

She looked at him from the corner of her eye and felt a flutter low down in her belly. His square jaw, gorgeous mouth and deep brown eyes were enough to make her body tremble with a need she hadn't felt since that long-ago night. She remembered it all so well. The soft touches, the hungry sighs, the frantic whispers. She could almost feel his hands on her skin again. His hard-muscled body covering hers, his heavy thickness sliding deep inside—

"So," he asked companionably, "how've you been?"

Sadie jolted, called herself an idiot and forced a smile. She wasn't going to have the conversation they needed to have while riding through town in his truck, so she stalled. "Fine, really. No complaints. How about you?"

"You know," he said with a shrug, "I'm good. Nice to be home for a while though."

A while?

"How long are you home for?" she asked.

"Trying to get rid of me already?" He shot her another quick look and steered the truck down Main.

"No," she said and half expected her tongue to fall off due to that whopper. "I was just curious. You haven't been around much the last few years."

"And how would you know that? Weren't you living in Houston?"

"Houston isn't the moon, Rick," she said. "I talk to friends. My brother. They keep me up on hometown news."

"Me, too," he said. "Well, not your brother. He and I never really were friends."

"True," she said and silently added they were even

less likely to be friends now, though Rick didn't know it yet.

"Joe Davis told me when you moved out."

Sadie smiled and nodded. Joe and Rick had always been close. Not surprising that the town's best mechanic had kept Rick up to date on things. She was more glad than ever that she had left Royal when she had. If not, Joe would have told Rick her big secret and heaven knew what might have happened then.

"He, uh, also told me about Michael. I'm sorry."

A twinge of pain rattled through her heart at the mention of her late brother. Michael Price had led a troubled life. Somehow, he had never been able to find happiness, but he'd always looked for it in the bottom of a bottle. Eight months ago, he had been driving drunk and driven off a cliff road in California. She would always miss her brother, but Sadie hoped that he had at least found the peace he had been searching for.

She lifted her chin. "Thanks. It was hard. Losing him like that. But I was grateful that he hadn't killed anyone else in that wreck," she said simply.

"He was a good guy," Rick said softly.

"He was a good brother, too," Sadie said, smiling sadly. Her memories of Michael were mostly good ones and she clung to them.

"And," Rick said, changing the subject, "now you've left Houston to come home again. You're living with your dad?"

"Just temporarily," she said. "Until I find a place of my own. Ever since Mom died several years ago, Dad spends most of his time on fishing trips. He's in the Caribbean now, and Brad doesn't live there anymore, so…"

"You're not lonely in that big place all by yourself?"

She nearly laughed. "No. It's fair to say, I haven't been lonely in a long time."

Rick frowned. "What's his name?"

"His? Who his?"

"The guy you're seeing," he countered. "The I'm-too-busy-to-be-lonely guy."

Sadie snorted. "There's no guy. Too busy for one of those, too." She left it at that, not bothering to explain what he would find out for himself all too soon.

Silence stretched out between them, the only sounds the crunch of the wheels against the asphalt and the soft sighing of the truck's air conditioner. Outside, summer sun beat down on Royal, Texas, making even the trees seem to slump with fatigue.

"You know," he said finally, "I seem to remember you being a hell of a lot friendlier the last time I saw you."

Oh, boy. She remembered, too. In fact, her memory was so clear and so strong, it was all she could do not to squirm in her seat. A flush of heat spread through her body as images rushed through her mind. His body. Hers. Locked together. Desperate kisses, amazing sensations. Didn't seem to matter that she was already so nervous she could hardly swallow. In spite of everything, Sadie knew that if he reached over to touch her right now, she would probably go up in flames.

"You okay?" he asked from beside her and that deep voice of his seemed to roll across her skin.

Oh, she really was *not* okay.

"Sure," she lied. "Fine."

The familiar scenery raced past them as he left town behind and drove along the highway toward the Price family mansion in the exclusive development of Pine Valley. Three years ago, Sadie had walked away from the home where she grew up to live in Houston, losing herself in the hustle and the crowds. At the time, she had definitely needed to get away. To find a fresh start where no one really knew her. Where her private life wouldn't be fodder for local gossips.

Now though, she was back and the past was reaching out to grab her.

She looked at Rick again. Funny, she'd known him most of her life and yet hadn't connected with him at all until that one, memorable night. He'd changed, she thought. He looked older, more serious, more self-confident somehow. And that was saying something, since Rick had never been lacking in confidence.

His brown hair was trimmed military short, his brown eyes locked on the road in front of them. His hands were wrapped around the steering wheel and she watched as the muscles in his arms flexed.

"You sure you're okay?" Rick asked, glancing at her briefly before shifting his gaze back to the road.

That was Rick, she thought. He wasn't the kind to be distracted from what he saw as his duty—which at the moment, was driving. He appreciated rules and order and as far as she knew, always did the "right" thing, whatever that might be at the time.

There was simply no way he would ever accept *her* version of "right." This day wasn't going to end well, yet Sadie couldn't find a way out of it. Now that she was home in Royal, people were going to talk. And the fact that Rick had only been home for a day was probably the only reason he hadn't heard whispers already.

Well, she couldn't let him hear this news secondhand. She owed him the truth. At last.

"Yeah, I'm fine." *Just trapped like a rat,* she added silently. Oh, she had known that this day was going to arrive, sooner or later. She had just been hoping for later.

Much later. Which was ridiculous really, she argued with herself. She had moved back to Royal. She knew that, eventually, Rick would return. And keeping a secret in a small town was just impossible. Wasn't that one of the reasons she had left in the first place?

Frowning, she focused on the road and tried not to think about what would happen when they got to her family home.

"If you say so," he said, his tone telling her he wasn't convinced. "So. Since you're fine and I'm fine and we're not talking about anything else, why don't you tell me what you were doing at the TCC besides making your brother crazy?"

She blew out a disgusted breath at the mention of her brother. "Shoe was on the other foot, actually. Brad is the most stubborn, hardheaded man in the state of Texas."

"This is news to you?" he asked with a chuckle.

Brad Price had long had the reputation in town of being the most hidebound traditionalist in the known universe. His hard head only added to the fun.

"No," Sadie said, grateful to have a safe subject to talk to him about. "But I keep hoping that somehow, someday, Brad will wake up in the twenty-first century. Anyway, I went in to talk to him about being a part of designing the new clubhouse."

"There's going to be a new clubhouse?" Rick whistled, long and low. "Never would have believed that. The club's been the same for more than a hundred years."

Sadie rolled her eyes and shook her head. "So it should always stay the same? Why put in electric lights? Why aren't they still using oil lamps or candles? Why have a telephone? Is tradition so important that no one wants progress?"

"Whoa!" He laughed, then asked, "Is progress so important you just forget about tradition?"

She glared at him, those warm, sexy feelings she'd been experiencing only moments ago dissolving as surely as sugar in hot coffee. "You sound just like Brad. Is this a guy thing? Is it only women who are willing to look at the future?"

"No, but looking to the future doesn't mean forgetting the past."

"Who said anything about forgetting?" Sadie waved her hand in dismissal. "All we're talking about is an up-to-date, comfortable club that *every* member can enjoy."

"Now I know what this is about." He smiled and nodded sagely. "I heard Abby Langley's a member now. I suppose that's what's got the women in town up in arms?"

She just stared at him. "Is it all men or just *Texans?*"

"Huh? What?"

"You have that drawling tone to your voice when you say 'women' like you're describing a child throwing a tantrum."

"Hold on a minute, I wasn't trying to start a fight."

"No, you're just stuck in the same rut every other man in town is in."

"I've been home for a day and suddenly I'm the enemy?"

"No," she said on a sigh. "You just caught me at a bad moment. Sorry."

He shrugged. "No problem. I know what it's like to be up to your eyeballs in something and take it out on someone else."

"Still not much of an excuse. It's just that Brad makes me so furious."

"Isn't that what brothers are for?"

"I suppose so," she acknowledged, then she smiled. "Besides, I think Brad having to deal with Abby is going to be payback enough."

"Who knew you had such a mean streak?" he asked, his grin taking the sting out of his words.

"I'm a Price, too, don't forget."

"Wouldn't dare." He steered into a left turn lane and stopped for the red light. "I've done a lot of thinking about you in the last few years, Sadie."

"You have?" She tensed up again. What was it about this man that could set every nerve in her body to jangling?

His long fingers tapped against the steering wheel. "Sometimes, thoughts of you were all that kept me sane."

"Rick…"

"You don't have to say anything," he said. "I just wanted you to know that the night we had together has stayed with me."

"It stayed with me, too," Sadie said, then turned her head to avoid his gaze.

That single night with him three years ago had changed her life so completely, it was no wonder that she'd thought of him often. But now, knowing that he had been doing the same, made her feel even more of a terrible person than she had been. What could she possibly say to him? How would she ever explain?

She'd spent a lot of time assuring herself that one day, she'd tell him everything. That when he got back she would apologize and do whatever she could to make things right.

Yes, she could have written to him, but she had talked

herself out of that. She'd been...worried about him. A career marine, he had been in harm's way for most of the last few years, and every night, she'd said a prayer for his safety. If she had told him the truth in a letter, it might have distracted him when he could least afford it. Besides, a letter would have been the coward's way out. Face-to-face was the only honorable way. And like she said, Sadie was a Price, too. Her parents had raised their children to be honest, to keep their word and to never break a promise. Honor meant something to the Price family.

But that didn't mean that she had room for him in her life. She wasn't looking for a husband. She didn't need a man, her life was busy enough at the moment, thank you very much. But she did owe him the truth.

And that was something she wasn't looking forward to.

He pulled to a stop at a red light, then turned his head to give her a quick grin. Only one corner of his mouth tipped up, and in that instant, Sadie felt a flash of heat wash over her. Just like it had on their one and only night together three years ago.

"So tell me what you did in Houston."

She eased back into the seat. "I did a lot of charity work. The Price family foundation is based in Houston," she said with a lift of her shoulders. "And I served on the board of my father's art museum."

"You enjoyed that?"

She looked at him. "Yes, but..."

"But?"

"But, I always wanted to go into design. Landscape design, really." She turned to face him. "Planning out gardens, parks, working with the city to fix the roads along the highways..."

When he just stared at her, Sadie stopped talking and shrugged. "It just appeals to me."

"You should do it then," he told her. "Go take classes. Learn. Doing what you love is what makes life worth living."

The light changed and he drove on.

"Is that why you're still a marine?"

He laughed. "There's an old saying—*once a marine, always a marine.*"

"Yes, but you're still active duty. Why?" She was watching him closely, so she noticed when his jaw tightened slightly. "You could come back to Royal, run your family ranch. Why stay in the Corps?"

"Duty," he said simply. "It's an old-fashioned word, but I was raised to take it seriously. My father was a marine, you know."

"Yeah, I know."

"We traveled all over the world when I was a kid. Finally settled here when he left the Corps, because my mom had roots here." He glanced at her. "But when you grow up on bases, when you see what people are willing to give to serve their country… Well, it makes you want to do the same. And by doing my duty, serving my country, I help keep everyone I care about safe."

She felt a sting of tears in her eyes and frantically blinked them back. Here he was talking about honor and duty and she had been lying to him for nearly three years. She was a rotten human being. She deserved to be flogged.

They drove down her street and suddenly Sadie had to say something. Try to prepare him for what he was about to find out.

"Rick, before we get to the house, there's something you should know—"

"If it's about the flamingos, I've got to say that maybe you should rethink landscape design."

"What?"

Grinning, he pulled into the driveway and that's when Sadie noticed the flock of pink plastic birds on the front lawn. Thank heaven her father was off on his fishing trip. If Robert Price had seen his elegant lawn covered with the tacky pink birds, he—well, Sadie wasn't sure what he'd have done, but it wouldn't have been pretty.

"Oh, for heaven's sake." As soon as Rick parked the car opposite the front door, Sadie hopped out and walked around the hood. She crossed the front yard until she came to the closest flamingo. The birds were staggered across the expertly trimmed lawn and looked so ridiculously out of place, Sadie couldn't help laughing.

"What's this about? A new trend in decorating?"

She jolted when Rick came up behind her. As hot as the July sun felt on her skin, his nearness made her temperature inch up just that much higher. There had never been another man in her life who had affected her like Rick Pruitt did. Not even her ex-husband-the-lying-cheating-weasel.

She took a breath, steadied herself, then looked up at him, trying not to fall into those dark brown eyes. It wasn't easy. He was tall and muscular and even in his jeans and T-shirt, Rick looked like a man used to giving orders and having them obeyed.

He was the quintessential Texas man. Add the Marine Corps to that and you had an impossible-to-resist combination. As the quickening heat in her body could testify.

Swallowing hard, Sadie fought past the dry mouth to say, "Actually, the flamingos are a fundraising drive for a local women's shelter." She tore her gaze from his and scanned the fifty or more pink birds scattered across the yard and sighed. "Summer Franklin runs it."

"Darius's wife?"

"Yes. The idea is that whoever receives the pink flamingo flock pays the charity to remove them and pass the birds onto the next 'victim'. Then that person pays and so on and so on…"

Rick laughed, pulled up one of the flamingos and looked it dead in its beady eye. "Sounds like a fun way to make money for a good cause."

"I suppose," she said, and worriedly looked at the hot-pink birds. "But they're so tacky. I'm just grateful my father's not here. He'd have a fit, wondering what the neighbors would be thinking."

Shaking his head, Rick stabbed the flamingo's metal pole back into the lawn and looked at Sadie. "Now that sounds like the prim and proper Sadie Price I used to know. Not the woman I spent that night with."

Prim and proper.

That's how she had lived her entire life. The perfect Price heiress. Always doing and saying the proper thing. But that, she assured herself, was in another life.

"I'm not that girl anymore, believe me." She looked up at him again and said, "Can you come in for a minute? There's something you need to see."

"Okay." He sounded intrigued but confused.

He wouldn't be for long.

She headed for the front door, let herself in and almost sighed with relief as the blissfully cool air-conditioned room welcomed her. A graying blonde woman in her fifties hurried over to her. "Miss Sadie, everything's fine upstairs. They're sleeping like angels."

"Thanks, Hannah," she said with a smile, not bothering to look back at Rick now. It was too late to back out. Her time had come. "I'll just go up and check on them."

The housekeeper gave Rick a long look, shifted her gaze to Sadie and smiled. "I'll be in the kitchen if you need anything."

Rick pulled his hat off and waited until Hannah was gone before he spoke. "Who's asleep? What's this about?"

"You'll see." She still didn't look at him, just walked across the marble floor toward the wide, sweeping staircase. "Come on upstairs."

She slid one hand across the polished walnut banister as she climbed the steps. Her heart was racing and a swarm of butterflies were taking flight in the pit of her stomach.

"What's going on, Sadie? In town, you said we had to talk. Then you say I've got to see something." He stepped around her when they reached the second-floor landing and blocked her way until she looked up at him. "Talk to me."

"I will," she promised, finally staring up into his eyes, reading his frustration easily. "As soon as I show you something."

"All right," he told her, "but I never did care for surprises."

The thick, patterned floor runner muffled their footsteps as they walked down the long hallway. Every step was more difficult than the last for her. But finally, she came to the last door on the left. She took a breath, turned the knob and opened it to a sunlit room.

Inside were two beds, two dressers, two toy boxes. And sitting on the floor, clearly not sleeping like angels, were her twin daughters.

Rick's twin daughters.

The girls looked up. Their brown eyes went wide and bright and they smiled as they spotted their mother. Sadie dropped to her knees to swoop them into her arms. With her girls held tightly to her, she turned her gaze on a stupefied Rick and whispered, "Surprise."

Three

Rick felt like he'd been kicked in the head.

Twin girls.

With *his* eyes.

They were jabbering nonstop as they climbed over their mother.

Their mother.

Sadie Price was the mother of *his* daughters.

Shock slowly gave way to an anger that burned inside him with the heat of a thousand suns. He was blistered by it and forced to contain it all because damned if he'd lose his temper in front of his children.

The girls were wearing matching pink overalls with pink-and-white checked shirts. Tiny pink-and-yellow socks were on their impossibly small feet and they laughed and danced in place as Sadie held on to them.

Sadie's gaze locked with his and he read her guilt in her eyes. Her regret. Well, it was a damned sight late for regret. She'd kept his daughters from him their whole lives.

There would be payment made.

For now though, he dropped to one knee and looked at the girls. Their brown hair curled around their heads, their cheeks were pink and their brown eyes sparkled with life. Love. His heart clenched hard in his chest. One of the girls looked at him warily, and then slowly gave him a smile that tore up his insides.

"Girls," Sadie said, laughing as the twins continued to chatter a mile a minute.

"Birds, Mommy."

"Lots."

"I know," Sadie said, giving first one of her daughters then the other a big kiss. "I saw them."

"Pretty."

"Yes, they are pretty," Sadie agreed.

"Who him?"

Who him. Rick swallowed back the tight ball of anger lodged in his throat. His daughters didn't know him. He was a damn stranger to his own flesh and blood. That knowledge hurt more than he would have thought possible.

"This is your daddy," Sadie said, watching him as she spoke the words that made all of this a reality.

He sat down, drew one knee up and rested his forearm on it. He wasn't going to crowd the little girls. But he wanted more than anything to hold them. Instead, he smiled. "You are the prettiest girls I have ever seen."

The one closest to him gave him a sly smile and looked up at him from beneath lowered lashes that lay like black velvet on her cheeks. Oh, this one was going to be a heartbreaker when she grew up.

"Daddy?" she said and pushed away from Sadie to walk to him.

Rick's heart stopped as she approached him. He was afraid to move. He worried that anything he did now might shatter the moment. And he didn't want to risk it. When she was close enough, the little girl reached out and patted his cheek. Her small hand was feather-soft against his skin and she smelled like shampoo and apple juice.

"Daddy?" She leaned in to give him a hug and Rick held her as carefully as he would have a live grenade. This tiny girl, so perfect, so beautiful, had accepted him without reservation and he'd never been more grateful.

"Daddy!" The second twin rushed him, cuddling up to him just as her sister had and Rick closed his eyes and wrapped his arms around them. He held them close, feeling the warmth of their bodies, the fluttering of their heartbeats. And in one all-encompassing instant had his life, his world, altered forever.

Opening his eyes, he looked at Sadie and saw that she was crying. A single tear rolled down her cheek as she watched him with their children and he asked himself what she was crying for. Was she pleased that he was finally meeting his daughters? Or was she regretting telling him at all?

"Story!" One of the girls blurted the word and pushed away from him, running to a bookcase beneath the window. Meanwhile, her twin settled in on Rick's lap and played with his hat.

"How old are they?" he asked tightly.

"You know exactly how old they are," Sadie whispered.

"What are their names?" That question cost him. He didn't know the names of his children. His heart was being ripped into pieces in his chest and there didn't seem to be a damn thing he could do about it.

Sadie scooted closer to them, reaching out to fix a sliding pink barrette in one of the twins' soft, wispy hair.

"This one is Wendy," she said, dropping a kiss on the girl's nose.

"Wenne!" the toddler repeated with a gleeful shriek. She put her father's hat on and the Stetson completely swallowed her head. Her giggle was as soft as a summer wind.

"Wendy has freckles on her nose."

"Nose!"

Smiling, Sadie captured the returning twin and swooped her up into her lap. She kissed the top of the child's head and met Rick's eyes when she said, "This one is Gail."

Another surprise in a morning full of them.

His heart, which he would have sworn had already been ripped in two, shredded even further as he looked down at the smiling child on Sadie's lap. He actually felt a sharp sting of tears in his eyes and swiped one hand across his face to rid himself of them. Only then did he trust himself to look at Sadie again. "You named her for my mother."

"Yes," she said as the little girl opened the storybook and started "reading" to herself.

"Doggie and a bug and running and..."

Her commentary went on, but Rick hardly heard the mumble of disjointed words and phrases. He was caught in the moment. Struggling hard for the rigid self-control he had always been able to count on.

But he would challenge any man to walk into a situation like this one and not be shaken right down to the bone.

"Gail has a dimple in her left cheek that Wendy doesn't have." She smoothed one hand over her daughter's hair. "And Gail's hair is straighter than Wendy's. When you get to know them, you'll see other differences, too. Their personalities are wildly different."

"Sadie…"

"Wendy is the adventurer. She was getting into things the minute she could crawl," Sadie said, her words coming faster and faster, as if she didn't want to give Rick a chance to say anything. "Gail is the cuddler. Nothing she likes better than curling up on your lap with a book. But she's no pushover, either. She holds her own with her sister and, honestly, the two of them are so stubborn that sometimes…"

"Sadie," he said, his voice deeper, more commanding.

She blew out a breath and slowly lifted her eyes to his. "I know what you're going to say."

"Oh, I don't think you can even guess what I want to say," he told her, anger rippling just beneath the surface of his voice.

"Let me explain, all right?"

"Can't wait to hear it," he assured her, though Rick knew there was absolutely nothing she could say that would make what she had done okay.

He'd been cheated out of his daughter's lives.

Wendy pushed his hat off her head and left him for her mother. Both girls were in Sadie's lap as she read them a story. Their laughter filled his heart even as he struggled with the fury he felt toward their mother.

As he watched her with them, he saw a completely different Sadie than the one he knew. He'd always seen her as an untouchable princess. Born and raised to be the perfect southern lady. Until their one night together, he would have been willing to bet that Sadie Price had never done a damn thing that was even remotely undignified.

Yet here she was now, on the floor, cuddling with two babies like she didn't have a care in the world.

"Daddy! Story!" Wendy reached out a tiny hand to him and Rick's aching heart did a flip-flop in his chest. He would have his answers, he promised himself. But for now, he wanted to make up for lost time. He wanted to be with his children.

And the woman who had kept them from him.

He moved in closer, taking Wendy onto his lap and the four of them became a unit while Sadie's voice wove threads of family around them.

An hour later, the girls were asleep and Sadie and Rick stepped into the hall. She was so tense she was half afraid her spine might snap.

"You just leave them alone up here?" Rick asked as Sadie quietly closed the door behind her.

"There's a baby monitor in the room with receivers downstairs and in my room. I can hear everything that goes on in there."

He nodded and gripped the brim of his hat so tightly his knuckles went white. Sadie could feel anger radiating from him and the worst part was she couldn't blame him for any of it. What man wouldn't be furious to suddenly be faced with the fact that he was a father and hadn't been told about it?

"I think it's time you and I had that talk," Rick said, taking hold of her elbow to steer her down the hall and away from their daughters' bedroom.

"Let's go downstairs, then," Sadie said, pulling free of

his grip. Yes, he had a right to be angry, but she wasn't going to be bullied. Not by anyone. Never again.

She walked ahead of him, head held high, and took the stairs at a brisk clip. Once downstairs, she turned and walked into the family living room. "Have a seat. I'm going to ask Hannah for some iced tea. Do you want anything?"

"Just answers."

"You'll get them." He wouldn't like them, she thought as she walked through the house to the kitchen. But she couldn't help that. What was done was done and they'd just have to go forward from here.

In the cavernous kitchen, Hannah was sitting at a table with a cup of tea and a plate of cookies. "Miss Sadie. Did you want something?"

"Just some iced tea please, Hannah. And some of those cookies if you've got extra."

Hannah grinned. "With those two little angels in the house? I always have spare cookies. You just go on out to the front room. I'll bring it along."

Sadie turned for the door, then stopped as Hannah asked, "Is your friend still here? Would he like some as well?"

"Yes, thanks Hannah. Tea for both of us." As she walked back to the living room, Sadie told herself giving Rick something cold to drink, whether he wanted it or not, might just help cool him off.

Back in the living room, she found him standing at the bank of windows overlooking the front lawn. The pink flamingos looked so silly, she almost smiled. Until Rick turned to give her a glare that could have brought snow to Dallas.

"Start talking," he said thickly, tossing his hat to the nearest chair.

"It's a long story."

"Cut to the part where you give birth to my children and don't bother to tell me."

"Rick, it's just not that simple."

"Sure it is. Lies aren't complicated. It's living with them that makes things tough." He shoved both hands into his jeans pockets. "Though you've managed to do it just fine for nearly three years."

Sunlight streamed into the room and lay across glossy wood floors. Scatter rugs dropped splotches of color in the room and the oversize sofas and chairs gave a cozy feel in spite of the chill she was feeling from Rick. This had always been her favorite room in her family's home. Though now, she had the feeling she would never again walk into it without seeing Rick's accusatory stare.

Sighing, she bent to the baby monitor sitting on a side table and turned up the volume. Then she walked to him and stopped in a patch of sunlight, hoping the warmth would ease some of the cold she was feeling. Rick stood his ground, as immovable as a mountain. He was tall and broad and, right now, he looked like fury personified. His brown eyes flashed with banked anger and his shoulders were so stiff, she could have bounced a quarter off the tendons in his neck.

"You should have told me," he said flatly.

"I wanted to."

"Easy enough to say now."

"Nothing about this is easy, Rick," she countered and wrapped her arms around her middle. She took a deep breath and then continued. "You weren't here, remember? You left the day after we—"

"—made twins?" he finished for her.

"Yeah." Sadie had thought about this moment so many times, she'd even practiced what she would say.

How she would explain. And now that the moment was here, her mind was a total blank.

"By the time I found out I was pregnant, you were in a war zone."

"You could have written," he argued. "My mother had my address. She knew how to get in touch with me."

"I know." Sadie rubbed her hands up and down her arms. "I went to see your mom, actually."

"You what?" He looked stunned.

"When I knew I was pregnant, I went to talk to your mother and—"

"Here we are," Hannah announced as she pushed a rolling cart carrying a pitcher of tea, two glasses filled with ice and a blue-and-white plate full of cookies.

She settled the cart in front of one of the matching sofas, then smiled at the two of them. "You just help yourselves, and don't mind the cart when you're finished, Miss Sadie. I'll come back to collect it later."

"Thank you, Hannah." Desperate for something to do, Sadie hurried to the cart and poured tea into both glasses. "Sure you don't want any?"

"No, thanks. And stop being so damn polite." He walked closer and waited for her to take a sip of her tea. "Why did you go see my mother?"

Sadie set the glass down, sorry now she'd had any. The cold she felt was deeper now, thanks to the icy tea sliding through her system. Looking into Rick's eyes didn't warm her any, either.

Sighing a little, she slumped onto the sofa and leaned back into the cushions. "Because I thought she had the right to know that I was pregnant with her grandchildren."

"She *knew?*" Those two words sounded as if they had been strangled from his throat. Rick shook his head and she knew he was even more shocked than he had been before. "My mother knew you were pregnant and even *she* didn't tell me?"

"We talked about it," Sadie said, turning toward him as he dropped onto the sofa beside her. "We both decided that it wouldn't be right to give you something else to worry about while you were on the battlefield."

He laughed and the short, sharp sound was brittle. "You decided. Between the two of you, you decided to keep this from me." Rick shook his head. "I don't believe any of this."

Sadie reached out and laid one hand on his arm. When he glared at her, she pulled back. "Don't you get it? Your mother was terrified for your safety. She'd already lost your father and the thought of losing you to war was killing her."

His jaw worked as though he was actually biting back words that were struggling to get out.

"She didn't want you distracted. Neither did I," Sadie said. "If you had known, you might have been less focused on what you needed to do."

"I had the right to know."

"We were trying to protect you."

He laughed again and this time Sadie actually winced at the sound.

"That's great. You and my mom protect me by hiding my kids from me. Thanks."

His features were hard and tight, his eyes still flashing with the anger she knew must be pumping thick and rich inside him.

"I know you're mad," she said.

"There's an understatement."

"But I still think we did the right thing," she told him.

"Yeah?" He turned on the sofa to glare at her. "Well,

you didn't. You should have told me. *She* should have told me."

"We were going to tell you," Sadie argued, "when you came home on leave. But—"

"—Mom died in that car wreck and instead of coming home for her funeral, I took R&R in Hawaii. I couldn't face coming back here with her gone."

"Yes."

He scrubbed one hand across his face, then rubbed the back of his neck. "I don't even know what the hell to say about all of this, Sadie." He glanced at her. "There's one more thing I need to know."

"What?"

"If we hadn't run into each other this morning were you ever going to tell me about my children?"

Now it was her turn to be angry. "Of course I would have. You'll notice the girls weren't afraid of you, right? It was almost like they knew you already?"

He frowned, but nodded. "Yeah, I noticed that."

"That's because I showed them your picture. Every day. I told them who you were. That you were their daddy. They knew about you from the first, Rick."

He swallowed hard and took a deep breath. "I don't even know if that makes it better or worse."

Pushing up from the sofa, he stalked across the room, then turned to stare at her. "You showed them pictures of me, but I was never there. Did they wonder why? Do kids realize more than we think they do?"

Sadie stood up, too. Absently, she noted the overloud ticking of the grandfather clock in the corner. It hit the quarter hour and a bell chimed and still the silence between Rick and her continued. When she couldn't stand it any longer, she spoke up. "You're here now. You can get to know each other. I'm not trying to keep your girls from you, Rick. I never was. I just—"

"You moved to Houston because of them, didn't you? Because you were pregnant."

"Yes." She lifted her chin to meet his eyes. She wouldn't apologize for how she'd handled the biggest upset of her life. She had done the best she could and had never once regretted getting pregnant. "I couldn't stay here. Not with the town gossips. I didn't want the girls to suffer because of decisions you and I made."

His frown deepened.

"I wanted a fresh start."

"But you're back in Royal. Why now?"

"It was time. I was…lonely. I missed my home. My family. I wanted the girls to know their grandfather and their uncle."

"And their father?"

"Yes."

"Not so worried about the gossips now? What changed?"

"Me," she said simply. "I love my daughters and I don't care what any gossip has to say. Anyone tries to hurt my girls and they'll have me to deal with."

"And me," he assured her.

She could tell he was having a hard time believing anything she said and she really couldn't blame him for his doubts. But the truth was she had had every intention of telling him. "Honestly, Rick. I was going to be right here in Royal, waiting for you—whenever you came home. I was going to tell you about the girls. I want them to know their daddy."

Shaking his head, he walked toward her, gaze never leaving hers. He moved quietly for such a big man and she sensed the tension still holding him in its grip. When he was near enough, he reached out and grabbed her upper arms, pulling her close.

Sadie felt heat radiating off his body and reaching into hers. Just the touch of his hands on her skin was enough to start small brush fires in her blood. Her heartbeat was thudding in her chest and her mouth was so dry she could hardly swallow.

His gaze moved over her features like a slow caress. And his eyes were still churning with too many emotions to count. "I want to believe you, Sadie."

She tipped her head back to meet his eyes. "You can trust me, Rick."

"That's to be seen. But first things first." He released her, braced his legs in a wide-apart stance and folded his arms over his chest. "There's only one thing to be done now."

A ripple of apprehension scuttled through Sadie and still she asked, "What's that?"

"We're getting married."

Four

"You are completely out of your mind." She took a halting step back, forgetting the couch was right behind her. She toppled onto the cushions, but it took her but a second to scramble back up.

Maybe he was. Rick could admit that getting married wasn't something he had even considered until just a moment ago. Not that he was against marriage—for other people. But as a marine, he had never wanted to go off and leave a wife and kids behind for months at a time. Not to mention the hazards of his job. Why risk making a wife a widow? Sure, it worked for a lot of guys, but he'd seen enough marriages either dissolve or end in grief to not want to take the chance.

Now, though, things were different.

"It's the only honorable thing to do," Rick said, gaze following her as she pushed past him to hurry over to the front window.

"Honorable? You think marrying someone you don't love is honorable?" She laughed, shook her head and pointed one finger at him when he started for her. "You just stay away from me, Rick Pruitt."

"Not a chance," he snapped. He'd been put through an emotional wringer in the last hour or so and damned if he was even seeing straight yet.

He was a *father*.

He had twin girls who had his eyes and their mama's mouth and he hadn't even known they existed a few hours ago. How was that even possible? A man should *know* when he's created a life. When he's got family in the world.

Until today, he had thought himself alone. With both of his parents gone now, he'd had no real reason to leave the Marines. The Corps was his family now, he had told himself. Hell, he hadn't even wanted to come back to Royal on leave. Being in the empty ranch house was… lonely. Too many memories. Too much silence. Still, he had done his duty, come home to check on things, make sure the ranch was still operating as it should.

If he hadn't come home…would he ever have learned of his daughters? Sadie claimed she would have told him, but how did he know that for sure?

"I think we both need a little space right now, Rick," she said stiffly. "Maybe you should go." At her side in a couple of long strides, Rick pulled her in close again and this time wrapped his arms around her to hold her in place.

"You just dropped a bomb on me, Sadie," he ground out. "And if you think I'm gonna walk away from that, you're the one who's crazy."

"I'm not asking you to walk away," she argued, squirming in his grasp, trying to break free of him. "I'm just saying we should take a break. Get our thoughts straight before talking again."

"I don't need time to think," he told her. "I know everything I need to know. You're trying to keep my girls from me. Again."

Her jaw dropped. "Didn't I bring you here? Introduce you to the girls? I want you to be a part of their lives."

"On your terms though," he said, reading the truth in her eyes. "Come and go when you say? Show up for appointed visitation? Damn it, Sadie, I'm their father. I want more than weekends."

"It doesn't have to be like that," she said softly.

"No, it doesn't." The very thought of being cut off from his children was like a knife in the gut to him. He'd already missed too much. He hadn't seen Sadie pregnant. Hadn't heard the first cries of his babies being born. Hadn't seen that first smile or heard that first laugh.

A man alone treasured the thought of family. He wasn't about to lose his chance at having one.

"We can be together." Nodding, he took a breath. "We're their parents. It's only right we be married."

"This isn't a Victorian novel," she argued. "We can coparent successfully even if we're not a couple."

"Coparent." He snorted and looked down at her with a derisive half smile on his face. "Tidy words. Keeping each parent in their place. Is that it? Sounds like it came straight out of a self-help book."

"What if it did?" Her gaze shifted from his. "It makes sense."

"Not to me," Rick said flatly, holding her close enough that her body heat slipped into his. She wriggled some more, but all she succeeded in doing was rubbing herself against him until he was as hard as stone and she was panting with her own needs.

As soon as she realized that he had noticed her reaction, she went completely still. Rick smiled. "I know you can feel what you do to me."

She still wouldn't look him in the eye, but her breathing was heavier and she had stopped trying to pull away.

"I know you're feeling the same things I am," he said, sweeping one hand down her spine to the curve of her behind.

She sighed, closed her eyes and whispered, "It doesn't matter what we feel."

He rubbed her bottom until she was nearly purring in his arms. Rick had discovered on their one night together that beneath the surface of the genteel, aristocratic Sadie Price, there beat the heart and soul of a very sensual woman. He had been thinking about nothing but her for three long years and now that he was holding her again, he didn't want to let her go.

Ever.

All he had to do was convince her to marry him. How hard could it be?

"Baby, we're good together. That's more than a lot of people have when they get married."

Instantly, her eyes flew open and she glared at him. Damn, Rick thought, the woman could turn on a dime and he was never ready for it.

"Do *not* call me 'baby,'" she told him, then added, "I'm not marrying you just because we were good in bed together."

"Fine," he argued, "marry me because we have two children."

"And I thought my brother was the most stubborn male on earth."

Rick shook his head and tried to bite back his own frustrations. Most women in her situation would be leaping at the thought of marriage. Sure, she didn't have to worry about money. He couldn't dangle his own wealth in her face as a lure, because she came from the same kind of hefty bank account he did. But he didn't care how much the world had changed, being a single mother was harder than having a partner to share the work and worry. Why couldn't she see that?

"This isn't about stubborn. This is about you and me and what's best for our daughters."

"And you think that the girls would be better off living with two people who don't love each other?"

Scowling, he let her go when she pushed at him again. "This isn't about love. It's about duty. Our duty to our children."

"Duty isn't a reason for marriage, either. Trust me on this, I know what I'm talking about."

"Fine. Leave duty out of it." Rick shoved his hands into his pockets to keep from reaching for her again. "If we're married, we'll love the girls. That will be enough to build a family."

"No," she said with a harsh laugh. "It isn't enough. I'm not going to marry a man who doesn't love me. Not again."

She backed up a step or two, still shaking her head so firmly, Rick wasn't sure which one of them she was trying to convince.

"If you're talking about that moron you were married to for all of fifteen minutes…" he said.

"It was seven months and ten days," she countered hotly, her blue eyes flashing with the kind of heat that could fry a man. "Seven months before I actually *caught* him cheating on me. I found out later from my 'friends' that he'd been cheating on me all along, but nobody wanted to tell me."

"Don't you compare me to that piece of—" He caught himself and broke off. Then he moved in on her again, stalking her like a cat would a bird. "I don't cheat. And I don't lie. If I make a promise to a woman, I keep it."

"Good for you," she snapped. "I'm still not going to marry you."

Exasperated, he threw both hands high and let them drop. "Why the hell not?"

"I just told you," she muttered, keeping her voice low enough that Hannah wouldn't overhear their argument. "I married Taylor Hawthorne because it was *expected* of me. It was for the family. Good for business," she said and her mouth screwed up as if even the words tasted bitter. "I did what I was told. My father wanted me married, so I married. I was raised to do the right thing. To take one for the team," she said snidely. "To do my duty for the Price family. Well, no more. This is *my* life and I'll do with it what I damn well please."

She was shuddering by the time she stopped talking. Her breaths were coming fast and hard and there were unshed tears glittering in her eyes. Rick felt for her. He'd always known the Price family was far too interested in how things looked. When she married that no-account Hawthorne, Rick had assumed she simply had god-awful taste in men. But damned if he would have guessed that Sadie had laid herself down on a sacrificial altar for the sake of her father.

"I can understand how you're feeling, Sadie. Pisses me off just hearing it, so I imagine living it was that much worse. But it doesn't change a thing."

Stunned, she simply stared at him in confusion. "What?"

"We had children together, Sadie. We should be married." He moved closer, every step small and stealthy. Then he played his ace in the hole. He said the one thing he knew might sway her to accept his proposal. "I don't want my girls being called bastards. Do you?"

"Of course not!" She shook her head and chewed at her bottom lip and he knew he'd gotten to her with that.

The thought of anyone calling his babies names was enough to make him see red. But he knew as well as Sadie did that life in a small town wasn't always pretty. People would talk. Children would overhear it and they would repeat what their parents said.

He didn't want his girls paying for his mistakes.

"But I don't want to get married just for their sakes, either," Sadie said, her voice hardly more than a sigh. "That's not exactly a recipe for happiness, Rick."

A more stubborn woman never drew breath, he thought and swooped in on her, unable to keep from touching her for another minute. If he couldn't sway her to his point of view with logic, then damn it, he'd use whatever weapons he had in his war chest.

He wrapped his arms around her waist and pulled her so close she couldn't help but feel again his body's reaction to her. She wasn't immune to the chemistry sizzling between them. He could feel her heartbeat racing.

She closed her eyes, sighed a little and still shook her head. "No."

"Think about it, Sadie," he murmured, dipping his head to run his lips along the column of her throat.

She shivered and, damn it, so did he. The taste of her filled him. Her scent clouded his brain and shot his body into overdrive. His brain was fogging over and his instincts were clamoring at him to toss her down onto that so-comfortable sofa and lose himself in her. As he'd dreamed of doing for too damn long.

This woman had been in his soul—his bones— for as long as he could remember. Even as a kid, he'd noticed her. Now, as a man, he could admit that though he wouldn't love her, wouldn't love anyone, he felt more for her than he ever had for anyone else.

That would have to be enough.

She moaned, a small sound sliding from her throat as she clung to him, arching into his body with a need that matched his own.

"Remember that night?" he whispered, mouth moving over her throat, up to the line of her jaw and back down again. "How good it was? How good we were? We could have that again, Sadie.…"

She cupped his head in the palm of her hand and held him to her as she sighed in pleasure. He ran the tip of his tongue across her skin and nibbled at the throbbing vein at the base of her neck.

"I want you so badly I ache with it," he admitted. "And you want me, too. I can feel it."

"I do," she murmured and he felt a flicker of hope rise up inside him.

"Just think about marrying me, Sadie," he said softly, lifting his head to look down at her.

She swayed a little, opened her eyes, met his and stiffened. "That was so not fair," she muttered.

"Fair?" he countered. "You're the one holding all the cards here, Sadie. I'm just playing the hand you dealt me."

"Oh, stop with the poor-country-boy act," she told him, pushing out of his embrace to glare at him. "You knew exactly what you were doing. You were trying to seduce me into marriage and it's not going to work."

"Why the hell not?"

Sadie smoothed her hair, lifted her chin and said, "Good sex isn't enough to build a marriage on."

"It was *great* sex and it's a lot better than bad sex."

"I am not getting married."

"You surely are."

"You can't force me."

She had him there. He couldn't force her to marry him. But that wasn't saying that he wouldn't do his damnedest to convince her.

Gritting his teeth, Rick took a breath. "You know how you said earlier that Brad was a hardhead? Well, honey, you could give lessons."

"You've been back home one day, Rick. You told me yourself you're only here for a month."

True, he did have only thirty days' leave. But if he decided to get out of the Corps, he could be back in Royal in no time. To stay.

"I'll retire," he blurted the words, surprising even himself.

"Rick, you love being a marine. You told me so yourself not two hours ago." She stared up at him. "What about your duty to country?"

"I have a duty to my kids, too," he argued.

"God, what am I going to do with you?"

"Easily enough answered," he told her. "Marry me."

"Well," a voice said from the hallway, "it's about damn time."

Rick turned to face the man standing in the open doorway of the living room. Brad Price looked grim and his gaze was narrowed and fixed on Rick.

"Brad," Sadie said with a tired sigh, "what're you doing here?"

He came into the room, never taking his eyes off of Rick as he spoke to his sister. "I came to talk to you. Felt bad about our argument at the club."

"Now's not a good time," Sadie said quickly.

"Yeah, I can see that." He walked up to Rick, ignoring Sadie completely. "So you've seen the girls?"

"I have," Rick said, stepping forward and sweeping Sadie to one side of him, keeping his body between her and her brother. This was between him and Sadie and he wasn't about to let Brad push his way into the mix.

"You know," the other man said, "I agreed with Sadie when she decided not to tell you about the girls when you were overseas...."

"Big of you to agree with her to keep my kids from me."

"Brad," she said.

"She did it for you," Brad reminded him.

"Everybody's so thoughtful," Rick said, features hard and tight. "Doing me favors I never asked for. Hiding my children for my own good."

Brad took a step forward. "You ungrateful—"

Rick took a step closer. "You expect me to *thank* you?"

"Stop it," Sadie warned.

"What she did is between Sadie and me," Rick told the man staring him down. "Just like this conversation is. You don't get a vote."

"I'm her brother."

"Which is why I'm still being polite."

Brad's gaze narrowed, but Rick wasn't intimidated. He'd been through firefights, walked down dark streets in enemy territory. He'd had friends die in his arms and been convinced that he wouldn't live to see another sunrise. Nothing Brad Price could show him was going to throw Rick.

"I want to know what you're going to do about my sister and her daughters."

"Brad, honest to God, if you don't get out of here…"

"I'm not going anywhere until he tells me he's going to marry you."

"Not that it's any of your business, but I've already asked her. Twice. You walked in on the second time."

Brad nodded. "Good. When's the wedding?"

"Ask your sister."

Brad looked at her. "Well?"

Sadie stood to one side, arms crossed over her chest, the toe of her shoe tapping frantically against the wooden floor. "There's not going to be a wedding."

"Are you kidding me?" Brad looked at his sister as if he couldn't believe what he was hearing, and Rick was glad to see that someone else was as frustrated with her as he was. "He's finally home and wants to do the right thing by you and his kids and you tell him no? What are you thinking?"

She narrowed her eyes on him. "I'm thinking, Bradford Price, that this is a private argument and none of your business."

"None of my business?" he shouted. "You're my sister, how is this not my business?"

"Don't shout at her," Rick said, his own voice loud enough to command attention.

"Who the hell do you think you are?" Brad demanded, crowding in on Rick.

"I'm the man who's going to marry your sister and you'll watch how you talk to her from here on out."

"Is that right?"

"Damn straight," Rick told him, bristling for a fight. He hadn't come here looking for trouble, but he wouldn't walk away from it, either.

"I don't need you to defend me," Sadie said, turning on Rick with the same vehemence she'd shown to her brother only a moment ago.

"What you need is somebody to talk some sense into you," Brad snapped.

"Amen to that," Rick acknowledged, hating to agree with Brad on anything.

Miss prim-and-proper Sadie Price reached up, and tugged at her own hair in sheer frustration. Letting her hands fall to her sides again a moment later, she shot a glare first at her brother then at Rick. "I've had enough. I'm done talking. That's it. Both of you get out."

Rick dug in his heels. "He can go. I'm not finished."

"Yes, you are."

"Why should I go?" Brad demanded. "This is my house, too."

"Not anymore. Go away," Sadie repeated. "Both of you."

"Sadie, you're not being reasonable," Rick said stubbornly. "We're not finished talking."

"Thank God one of you is making sense," Brad muttered.

"I'm with Sadie on this one, Price," Rick said tightly. "Butt out."

"*Both* of you butt out," Sadie snapped.

"I swear the women in this town are ruining men's lives." Clearly disgusted with his sister, Brad shook his head. "Abby Langley's driving me around the bend and here you are doing the same thing to this poor bastard."

Sadie poked him in the chest with her index finger. "Don't you swear at me." When Rick grinned, she turned on him in a flash. "And I don't want to hear one more word from you, either. Both of you…just get out of my house."

A soft cry sounded and Sadie turned instantly toward the baby monitor on a nearby table. Another halfhearted sniffle and cry came through loudly. At least one of the girls was awake.

"I have to go check on the twins," she said, heading for the doorway.

Rick was right behind her. Hearing that tiny cry had sent an arrow of something sharp and sweet shooting through him. "Are they all right?"

She stopped, looked up at him and put one hand in the middle of his chest to keep him from coming any closer. "They're fine." Then she shot her brother an irritated look. "They probably just heard their daddy and their uncle acting like jackasses."

When she left the room, she never looked back, only called out as she went, "You two can see yourselves out."

Rick looked over to Brad. "Well, that went well, thanks to you."

"Don't blame me if you're fool enough to try to talk sense to a woman," Brad shot right back.

Frustrated beyond belief, Rick grabbed his hat and tugged it on. He shot Brad another hard look and said, "This isn't over between me and your sister."

"I wish you luck with that," Brad muttered. "But I warn you. Sadie's changed since the twins came. Used to be you could predict how she'd react to something. Now…" He shook his head helplessly.

He had already noticed the changes in Sadie, Rick thought, and hadn't needed her brother to clue him in. There was a time when Sadie Price never would have lost her temper. It wouldn't have been ladylike. Her icy coolness had always attracted him for some reason. But Rick had to admit that the wild heat of her now was even more appealing.

A few minutes later, Rick was in his truck, looking up at the facade of the Price mansion. Everything in him urged him to stay. To batter away at Sadie's arguments until they evaporated like shallow creeks in high summer.

But, he thought, as he turned the key and fired up the engine, he was already learning something about Sadie. She was a woman a man would have to sneak up on. She had already dug her heels in, refusing to marry him and she wasn't likely to back down from that.

So, he'd have to seduce her. Charm her. Get her into bed and make love to her until she couldn't think straight.

Then he'd get her to marry him.

Five

The fireworks booth was doing a booming business.

Nothing like a small-town Fourth of July, Sadie thought with a tired smile. She'd missed this when she was living in Houston and now that she was home, she wanted to be a part of it all.

Which was why she was standing behind the counter explaining the finer points of whistling rockets and multicolored fountains to excited kids and their tired parents.

She tried to see past the crowd to where Hannah was watching over her napping twins. But there were just too many people in the town square. Seemed like every citizen of Royal had turned out for the festivities. The noise level alone was almost deafening. Between the crowd itself and the country-and-western band playing at the far edge of the square, peace and quiet would be hard to come by today. But then, who needed peaceful on the Fourth of July?

Summer heat sizzled every breath and the delectable scent of barbecue drifted on a lazy wind. Sadie was having a good time. In fact, the day would have been perfect. If not for thoughts of Rick Pruitt. The man was keeping her on edge, though she hated to admit it, even to herself.

True to his word, he was getting to know his daughters, dropping by the house every day during the last week, playing, reading stories, helping with bath time. And the girls were delighted with the attention. Both Gail and Wendy woke up every morning now asking when Daddy was going to come.

"How you doing, Sadie?"

"What?" She turned and smiled at Abby Langley. "Sorry, I was daydreaming, I guess."

"In this heat, maybe you're just hallucinating."

Sadie laughed and shook her head. "If only…"

Abby leaned one hip against the counter. Handing Sadie a bottle of cold water, she uncapped her own and took a long drink. "Boy, that's good. Okay, so who's the daydream about? A certain marine, I'm guessing."

Sadie took a grateful sip of the icy water and let it slide through her system. Even with the fans behind them stirring the hot July air, it was stifling in the fireworks booth.

"Hey, Abby," one of the other workers called out.

"Sadie and I are on a break," she answered.

"I could use one. Too much heat and too many thoughts," Sadie admitted. "And yes, your guess was right. All of those thoughts are about Rick."

Abby was one of the only people outside her immediate family who knew the truth about the twins' father. Sadie hadn't had many close friends in her life, so she treasured Abby and had really missed their friendship when she and the girls were living in Houston. Abby understood growing up in Royal as the daughter of wealthy parents. But she also knew what it was like to strike out on her own. She had made a dot-com fortune when she lived in Seattle, then come home to Royal to marry her high school sweetheart. Everything had seemed perfect for her.

Of course, nothing had turned out the way she'd expected. What ever did?

"Tell me," Abby urged.

Sighing, Sadie said, "He's been coming over every day. Spending time with the girls…"

"And this is a bad thing?"

"No."

One of the other workers in the booth reached past Sadie for a box of red sparklers. Sadie took Abby's arm and pulled her away a few steps. Lowering her voice, she continued, "It's not that I don't want him to get to know his daughters. They should have a father in their lives and they're already crazy about him—"

"I hear a 'but' in there somewhere."

"But," Sadie acknowledged with a nod, "what happens when he ships out again? He's home on leave. He's still a marine, Abby. Which means he's not staying in Royal. When he leaves, the girls won't understand. They'll just know their daddy's gone."

"Okay, that would be hard," Abby said as they both deliberately ignored the customers starting to stack up on the other side of the counter. "But isn't it still better for them to know him?"

"Yes, of course, it's just…"

"Confusing?"

"Extremely," Sadie said with a sigh. "You know, even when I was a kid, Rick Pruitt…confused me."

Abby laughed. "Sadie, when we were kids, all boys confused us. Hasn't changed much."

"No." A sad smile curved Sadie's mouth as she idly straightened a stack of Magic Wonder fountains. "But for you, it was different. Your family was rich, but they didn't keep you *separate* from everyone in town. Brad and I went to private academies, remember?"

She shrugged as if it didn't bother her, but it still did. When she was a girl, Sadie had wanted friends. She'd seen the other girls her age going shopping or sitting in the diner, laughing together or flirting with boys, and she had desperately wanted to be one of them. But except for Abby, she remained an outsider. Just as she had been for most of her life.

"True, you weren't around much," Abby mused. "Even when you were, your father didn't really like you hanging out at the diner with the rest of us."

Sadie laughed at the image. "The children of Robert Price didn't 'hang out.'" She took another sip of water and looked out over the crowd gathered in the square. "We didn't really belong in Royal, you know? Oh, born and raised here, sure, but we could only see the other kids on the weekends, so we never really built the kind of friendships here that everyone else had. Our father was too determined to keep us isolated for whatever reasons." She smiled, reached over to squeeze Abby's hand. "If not for you, I would have been miserable. It was hard on me, but in a way, I think it was even worse for Brad."

"In what way?"

Sadie pushed a stray lock of blond hair out of her eyes

and shrugged again. "I don't know, he was popular with the girls in town."

"Of course," Abby muttered. "He never did have any trouble attracting girls."

Sadie grinned. "He's my brother and he irritates me beyond all reason at times, but come on. He *is* great-looking."

"Maybe," Abby allowed.

Still chuckling, Sadie said, "Anyway, even though *most*—" she paused for a knowing look at Abby "—of the girls liked him, the guys in town weren't real thrilled with the 'rich guy' swooping in on the weekends."

"Yeah," Abby said softly, reluctantly. "I'd forgotten about that."

Sadie blew out a breath. "God, that sounds so whiny, doesn't it? Poor little rich kids.…"

"You're not whiny. Ever. So," Abby prodded, "tell me about Rick?"

Sadie smiled ruefully. "You remember, he was Mr. Popularity even then. Captain of the football team." She shook her head and called up the memory of a teenaged Rick Pruitt, and in response, she felt that odd fluttering in her stomach again just as she had then. "He wore jeans and boots and T-shirts and his hair was too long and his eyes were too dark and he looked like every girl's dream of a bad boy who was really a good guy."

"Yeah," Abby said, smiling with her. "I do remember Rick as a teenager. Pretty studly even then."

Smiling, she looked at Abby. "He would walk into the diner and every girl there would turn to look at him."

"Even you," Abby said.

"Me, too," she admitted, then laughed a little. "But he hardly knew me. Still, anytime he said hello, I'd start burbling and stammering. I felt myself blushing and couldn't stop it. Ridiculous, right?"

"Not really. We all acted like that as kids."

"Yes," Sadie said, "but I'm still doing it. The old Rick was pretty irresistible. Now, though, since those last tours of duty, he's…changed. Become more—I don't know, not closed down, because he's open and loving with the girls. But there's something about him that is shut away. Locked down. And that tears at me, Abby. Oh," she said, pausing to huff out a frustrated breath, "I don't know why he affects me like he does, but it's automatic. Rick Pruitt's around and my brain turns to mush and my body lights up like one of these skyrockets we're selling."

"So having him around all week was a little tough?"

"Just a little."

"I hear that," Abby said, looking past Sadie to frown. "Nothing's as easy as it should be."

Sadie turned to follow her friend's gaze and sighed when she spotted Brad walking through the crowd. "So, you're having a few issues with men right now, too, huh?"

"You know I love you, Sadie," Abby said, scowling at the oblivious man as he stopped to greet a friend. "But your brother sometimes makes me want to scream."

"He has that effect on women. Even his sister," Sadie admitted ruefully.

"Well, this woman isn't going to let him win. He's trying to ignore me at the TCC. Thinks because I'm an 'honorary' member, what I have to say shouldn't matter." Abby winked at her. "He's the most hardheaded man I've ever come across and arguing with him is like trying to talk sense to a wall. But, I don't give up easy and Bradford Price won't know what's hit him when I'm through with him."

Sadie grinned in solidarity. It was nice to know she wasn't the only female being driven slowly insane by a man. "Good to hear. Can't wait to see it."

"There's something else you should see right now."

"Hmm? What?"

Abby turned Sadie toward the counter. "Why don't you take care of this customer?"

Rick Pruitt leaned his forearms on the sun-warmed counter, looked through the screen at Sadie. "So, what kind of fireworks do you have?"

He was in uniform and Sadie felt her breath slide from her lungs in pure, female appreciation. He looked tall and strong and proud. The left side of his chest was covered with rows of colorful ribbons and a few medals glinted dully in the sunlight.

A couple of women walked past behind him and Sadie saw them giving him a slow once-over. Even though a spark of jealousy flared up inside her, she couldn't blame the women a bit. Rick was the kind of man that men wanted to be and women simply wanted. And when one corner of his mouth tipped up in a half smile, Sadie knew she was in very deep trouble.

Just as she had admitted only moments ago, she could actually feel her brain shutting down while her body kicked into high gear.

"Sadie?" he prompted, as if he knew exactly what she was thinking. "Fireworks? What kind are we talking about?"

It wasn't easy, but she managed to get a grip on her imagination and her hormones. "The usual kind. They're safe and sane and very pretty."

Then she sent a frown after Abby who walked away

chuckling. A second ago, she'd been thinking how much she had missed Abby when she was living in Houston. Now, her best friend had left her alone with the very man Sadie had been complaining about. The traitor. Looking back at Rick, she forced her brain to wake up and pay attention, then kept her voice brisk and businesslike.

"What can I get you? All of the proceeds go to the women's shelter."

"Ah," he said. "Like the pink flamingos."

"Exactly." And, Sadie knew that Summer's shelter would be getting a nice donation today, judging from how busy the fireworks stand was. "So, what do you need?"

"Now, that's a tricky question, Sadie," he said, voice dropping to a low rumble that only she could hear.

She couldn't stop the wave of heat that washed through her at the teasing, sexy note in his voice. Despite the crowds surrounding them, it was as if they were suddenly all alone. What was it about him that got to her so completely? Sadie felt as though every nerve in her body was standing straight up and trembling.

Sadie had never felt this way about any other man. Ever.

Certainly not the husband she had married for all the wrong reasons. In fact, up until that one night with Rick, Sadie had been half convinced that she was simply not *meant* to experience the tingling, overpowering pleasures that she read about in romance novels.

But in Rick's arms, she'd found more than she had ever thought possible. Now staring into those brown eyes of his, she was so very tempted to find it all again. He was temptation personified and she was pretty sure he knew it. As if he was aware of her thoughts, his eyes warmed and seemed to twinkle and that's when her breath caught in her lungs and a low, burning ache settled deep inside her.

Somehow, against all odds, she found the strength to rein in her hormones.

Her daughters' faces swam in her mind and that helped. The girls had Rick's eyes, sparkling with mischief. Her twins. The daughters she and Rick had made together on that passion-filled night.

Sadie wasn't a lonely single woman anymore. She couldn't just fall into bed with a man anymore, no matter *how* tempting. She was a mom. A mom who couldn't afford to start something with the father of her girls, because the only reason he wanted her now *was* their girls.

He was charming and attractive and truth be told, a walking orgasm waiting to happen. But if they didn't share two daughters, would he be trying so hard to seduce her? Sadie didn't think so.

Steeling herself, she smiled. "Did you want to buy some fireworks, Rick?"

One eyebrow lifted, but he nodded as if he understood that he wouldn't be drawing her into a flirtatious battle. "Sure." His gaze slipped past her to the shelves stocked with brightly colored boxes of fiery splendor. "Why don't you tell me what kind of fireworks the girls like?"

Her heart twisted. How sweet was that, she thought. He wanted to get something for his daughters to enjoy. Helplessly, she admitted that the one sure way to her heart was through her daughters. And no doubt, a cynical voice inside her whispered, he knew that very well. She ignored that little voice. "They're so little, this will be their first year actually seeing fireworks. I think they're going to be overwhelmed."

"I'm glad I'm here to see it with them," he said.

"I am, too."

"Are you?" he asked, sliding one hand across the counter to sweep beneath the screen to touch her fingers.

A quick bristle of sensation swept through her at his touch and she pulled her hand away. She was standing on a razor's edge here and one push either way was going to dissolve what was left of her balance.

"Of course I am," she said. "The girls will love having you here."

"That's a start," he said.

"Sadie," Abby asked, as she walked up with a smile, "everything okay?"

"Fine," she answered. "Abby, you remember Rick Pruitt."

"Sure. Nice to see you again. Love a man in uniform."

He grinned and Sadie's stomach did a quick flip-flop.

"That's just why we wear them, Abby. Marines like to please their women."

"Women?" Abby asked.

His gaze shot to Sadie. *"Woman,"* he corrected.

Then, as if he hadn't started a brush fire in her bloodstream, he pulled out his wallet. "Give me a few of those red, white and blue sparklers and a couple of the Fiery Fountains."

Getting busy, Sadie grabbed up his order, put it all in a bag and took his money.

"Keep the change for the shelter," he said.

"Thanks. The shelter appreciates it."

"Happy to help." His gaze was locked on hers.

She pulled in a deep breath and sighed. "Rick, what do you really want?"

"You already know the answer to that, Sadie."

Sadie searched for something else to say, but came up empty. What was there left to say? Hadn't they been talking circles around each other for a week now? Nothing had changed. He wanted to marry her for their daughters' sakes and she refused to get married for the wrong reasons. Again.

He picked up the bag and asked, "I'll see you later, then?"

"We'll be here for the fireworks show." Knowing how the girls would be excited to see him, she pointed off to the gigantic black oak that stood in the town square. "Hannah and the girls are over there if you want to say hello."

A wide smile creased his face. "Thanks. Think I will." His gaze shifted to Abby. "Nice to see you."

"Thanks, you, too."

When he walked off, Sadie watched him until he was swallowed up by the slowly moving crowd. Then she sighed and Abby nudged her in the ribs.

"What?"

"He's still gorgeous."

"Yeah?"

"He looks at you like you're the last steak at a barbecue."

"I know." That's just how she felt when he was around.

"So what's the problem?"

"He's not here to stay, Abby," Sadie said, resting one hip against the counter.

"You don't know that. Word is he's thinking about retiring."

"Maybe," she said, looking back over the crowd in the direction Rick went. "But even if he did stay in town, it isn't me he wants. It's his girls."

Abby laughed and dropped one arm around her shoulders. "Not what it looks like to me, Sadie. He's really into you. It's in his eyes."

"He just *desires* me. That's different."

"And could be fun."

She shook her head even though she was smiling. "Fun isn't on my schedule," she said sadly. "I'm a mom now. I have to do what's best for my daughters."

"And what exactly is that?"

"Wish I knew," Sadie whispered as Abby moved off to wait on another customer.

The rest of the day passed in a flurry of activity. There were rides for the twins, a small petting zoo and a country-fair-like atmosphere at the booths filled with pies and handmade crafts.

Sadie had as good a time as a woman could who was twisted into knots. Rick was there. All day. He carried the girls when they got tired, indulged them in ice cream and candy and Sadie could only hope their tummies were tough enough to handle all the sugar. Sadie should probably have drawn a few lines in the sand. Put a lid on sugar consumption at least. But Rick was so excited with his daughters and the girls were simply nuts about their daddy. She simply couldn't force herself to be the disciplinarian at the party when everyone was having so much fun.

They settled on the blanket beneath the tree for a late lunch. It was just the four of them since Hannah had found a group of friends among the crowd. While the girls ate bananas and mac and cheese, Sadie unwrapped the sandwiches Hannah had packed for her. She handed one to Rick.

When he took it, his fingers brushed hers and she gasped a little. He heard it and smiled. "Thanks."

"Don't thank me," she protested. "Hannah packed the lunch."

"I wasn't talking about the sandwich."

"Oh?" She looked at him as she reached over to hand Gail a cup of milk.

"I meant," he said, smoothing one hand over Wendy's dark brown curls, "thanks for sharing our girls with me today."

"You don't have to thank me for that, Rick," she said softly. Yes, he was confusing the hell out of her personally, but his obvious love for the twins warmed her heart. "They're your daughters, too. I want you to know them. I want *them* to know *you*."

He glanced from each of his daughters' tiny faces back to Sadie. Dappled shade danced across his face as the leaves of the black oak dipped and swayed in the sultry breeze.

"I appreciate that. I do." He took a bite of the sandwich, chewed and swallowed. "But I want more than the occasional day with them, Sadie."

"I know that." She picked up the sippy cup of milk Wendy toppled over and set it upright again. "But—"

"No buts about it, Sadie. They're my family. My blood."

"And mine," she reminded him.

"Yeah, which brings me back to my point."

She cut him off. Sadie wasn't going to give him the chance to talk marriage again. Sharing the twins wasn't enough of a reason to get married. She wouldn't take that step again unless she was in love. "I know what your point is, Rick, but I haven't changed my mind."

"Why the he—" he broke off, looked at the girls and gave a rueful smile. "Why the *heck* not? We were good together."

"Yes, for one night."

"Could be every night."

"Marriages aren't only lived in bed."

"Doesn't hurt."

She sighed. "Rick, we've been over this already."

"And will be again," he told her, his brown eyes locked with hers.

"What's the point?"

"We have kids."

"And we can both love them without being married to each other."

"We could be a family," he said softly.

And for one brief moment, that word seemed to reverberate inside her. She had always wanted a family of her own. It was the main reason she had agreed to go along with her father's plan when he married her off to Taylor. She had believed back then that even if a marriage hadn't started out for the right reasons that two people who wanted to badly enough could build something good.

But she'd found out soon enough that a marriage without love wasn't a marriage at all.

"It's a bad idea, Rick," she said finally and met his eyes.

"You don't know that."

She actually laughed and Gail looked up at her with a grin. "Oh, yes," she said, "believe me when I say I do."

"You can't use your marriage as a measure of what we could have."

"It's exactly what I should do," she told him firmly. "My marriage was a misery because there was no love there. I married him for all the wrong reasons and I paid a heavy price." She paused, looked down at her daughters, laughing and babbling to each other, and she felt a well of love fill her. Shaking her head, she looked at Rick. "This time, it wouldn't be only *me* paying the price. And I won't risk putting my girls into an unhappy home."

"You think I would risk that?" Rick picked up a piece of banana and handed it to Wendy. "I only want what's best for them."

"And I believe you," Sadie said. "We just disagree on what's best."

He laughed shortly. "You think you've got your mind made up about me," he said after a long moment, "but things change, Sadie."

"I'm not going to change my mind," she warned.

"Don't make statements that are going to be hard to back down from when I finally convince you to see things my way."

"Are you always this confident?"

"When I know I'm right," he assured her.

A squeal of sound shattered their conversation and had Sadie's ears ringing. Wendy cried for her mommy and Gail crawled to her father and scrambled up onto his lap.

The mayor stood on a hastily built stage at one end of the square. Tapping and blowing into a microphone, the feedback was loud enough to tear paint from walls.

"Sorry about that noise," the mayor said, "but I think we've got it whipped now."

The crowd stirred, then settled down as they waited for the inevitable speeches. Sadie's gaze slid to Rick. He had one arm wrapped around Gail's sturdy little body and jiggled her instinctively to keep her happy.

He did that so easily, Sadie thought with a sigh. He had stepped into fatherhood so smoothly, it was as if he had been with the twins since the beginning. And if he had, she wondered, how would things be different now?

Might they have already become the family he claimed to want?

"I know," the mayor called out, his voice echoing weirdly through the speakers, "that none of you came to listen to speeches..."

"That won't stop you, Jimmy," someone in the crowd shouted.

"That'll be enough outta you, Ben," the mayor chided with a smile. "I'll make this short. But since we're all here and since it's our country's Day of Independence, I wanted to take the time to honor a few of our own."

A ripple of applause skittered through the crowd. Hesitant, since no one was sure what the mayor was up to yet.

Then he let them all know.

"Rick Pruitt?" Mayor Jim called. "I know you're here son, so come on up to the stage, will you?"

Frowning a little, Rick set Gail down on the blanket. His features went dark and his eyes were suddenly shadowed. Dutifully, though, he shrugged, then walked through the other picnickers toward the stage. Meanwhile, the mayor went on with his small roll call.

"Donna Billings. Frank Haley and Dennis Flynn, you come on up here, too."

Sadie's gaze locked on Rick as he walked up the steps to take his place on the stage. The other people who had been called up stood alongside him, each of them in uniform. They all looked as uncomfortable with the attention as Rick did.

Then the mayor announced, "How about we give a big Royal round of applause for our very own finest. Let's thank them all for their service to us and our country."

As the gathered townspeople erupted into wild shouts and thunderous applause, Sadie felt a chill of pride ripple along her spine. From across the square, Rick's gaze locked with hers and she knew that he had been right. If she wasn't careful, he might just change her mind.

Six

During the next week, Rick got reacquainted both with the woman he had spent the last three years thinking about, and with his home.

The Pruitt ranch, under foreman John Henry's stewardship, had continued to thrive. The herd of beef cattle was healthy and growing, and the acreage set aside for raising grain was more productive than he had a right to expect. John had done a hell of a job and Rick was grateful. Knowing his home was in good hands had made it possible for him to follow his own dream of service.

Now, though, he was back and he had to decide for himself if his dreams hadn't changed. Evolved.

Rick's life was more full than he'd ever experienced before. He had once thought that being a marine was the toughest job on the planet. But that was before he became a father. For the last several days he had spent as much time with them and Sadie as he could. Every time he saw those twin smiles beaming at him, his heart wrenched in his chest. It was lowering to admit just how his daughters had him wrapped around their tiny fingers.

There was nothing he wouldn't do for them. Nothing he wouldn't face for them. Their smiles were a benediction. Their laughter the sweetest sound he had ever heard.

Rick had never really thought about becoming a father. And now that it had happened to him, he realized just what a responsibility it really was. Loving a child—a family—was an anchor he didn't believe professional soldiers could afford. That lesson had been brought home to him all too clearly on his last tour.

And the guilt that gnawed on him every second of every day was a constant reminder.

Now, though, he was looking at the situation from a whole different angle. There were two people in the world, alive and breathing because of him and Sadie. Those girls…they needed a father. They needed *him*.

His children should be able to depend on him. To know that he would be there for them. And how the hell could he do that if he was ten thousand miles away, slinking through a desert with a pack and a gun?

Then there was Sadie herself. His feelings for her went deeper than he wanted to admit, but damned if he'd ever call it love. Still, she was a part of him now, as much as the girls were, and he didn't know what the hell to do with that information.

Standing out on the ranch house's wide front lawn, he looked at the place where he'd grown up and felt a stab of affection. The heart of the house was more than a hundred years old. Built by the first Pruitt to settle here—back when Sam Houston was still in charge of Texas.

That small cabin had eventually been added on to with wood, stone and brick until the house itself had sprawled across the land, meandering weirdly with walls jutting out at odd angles. His mother had once told him that when she first saw the ranch house, she thought it had looked like an enchanted cottage. To cement that notion, Rick's father had added a stone tower to the end of the house for his wife to use as a sewing room.

Rick's gaze moved over that tower now and he half expected to see his mother standing in one of the windows waving at him. The fact that she never would again hit him like a fist to the chest. He hadn't been here when she died. Hadn't been able to say goodbye. And that would always haunt him.

Had he given up too much in service to his country? Was it time to step back and let others take over the duties he had always held so dear? Hard to know. Hard to choose which part of your heart to listen to.

Which was why being here was both a balm and a curse. Being on the ranch again fed his soul. Knowing that he might be leaving it again tore at him.

"You look like a man with a lot on his mind."

Rick turned to watch John Henry walk up to him. The older man was in his sixties, but stood as straight and tall as a man forty years younger. His hair was liberally streaked with gray and the moustache drooping over his upper lip was white as snow. The corners of sharp blue eyes was deeply grooved from too many years squinting into the sun and his skin was as tanned as old leather.

John Henry was as much a part of the ranch as Rick himself was. Maybe more so, Rick thought now, since the other man was *here,* taking care of business while he himself was running all over the world taking care of everyone else's concerns.

"Plenty to think about," Rick admitted.

"Anything you want to talk over?"

Rick smiled. John had been on the ranch since Rick was a kid. He was as close to a father as Rick had now and though he appreciated the offer, he didn't see any point in talking about things he hadn't gotten straight in his own mind yet.

"Nope."

"You always were the closed mouth sort," John mused and turned his gaze on the house, too. "It's a good place, you know."

"Yeah, I know."

"But a house needs people living in it. A family. Making memories. It's not good for a house like this to stand empty too long."

"Real subtle," Rick said with a half smile.

"No point in being subtle. If I've got something to say, I just come out and say it."

Rick sighed. John had been warming up to this for a week, he knew. "Let's hear it."

The older man scrubbed one hand across the back of his neck. "You know I was just as proud of you as your folks were when you joined the Corps."

"I know that."

"But that said," John told him quietly, "there's a time for leaving home and there's a time for coming back."

He frowned, shifting his gaze to his mother's window again. If he hadn't left the last time, he'd have been here when Sadie found out she was pregnant. He'd have been here for his mother before she died. Maybe she wouldn't have died.

But the world of ifs was a crowded one with too many possibilities and no changes. Looking backward only fed regrets and that didn't help a damn thing.

"I'm just saying," John continued, "your mom was

real excited to know that Sadie Price was going to have your baby."

Rick snapped him a hard look. "Mom told you?"

"'Course she told me. And Elena. Who the hell else did she have to tell?"

"How about *me?*" he demanded, as a spurt of anger shot through him. "I'm standing here wishing I'd been here for Mom. For Sadie. And now I find out that not only my mother knew about the twins, but you and Elena did, too? Don't you think somebody should have told me that I was going to be a father?"

John didn't even blink in the face of Rick's anger. Instead, he frowned. "Yeah, I did think you should be told. But your mother didn't want you distracted while you were over there. She about wore out her knees praying for you every night and she thought that if you knew about the babies that you wouldn't be focused and could end up getting hurt. Or worse."

The mention of his mother's prayers quelled the fiery anger inside him with a bucket of guilt as effective as ice water. But he had to ask. "When she died, why didn't you write and tell me about the girls then? I could have come home."

"For how long? A two-week leave? Then you head back to a combat zone? What would have been accomplished?" John shook his head and scraped one work-worn hand across a hard jaw covered with gray stubble. "No. Your mother was right not to tell you. Wasn't my call to go against her wishes."

"Fine," he muttered, realizing that this was an ancient argument and nothing would be changed by it, anyway. Besides, maybe John was right. Who the hell knew? He could admit that finding out about his mother's death while he was overseas hadn't been an easy thing. Discovering the truth about the girls might have been even harder to take. "Doesn't matter anymore, anyway. Point is, I'm home now. I know about the twins, now."

"Yeah. The question is, what're you going to do about it?"

"Wish I knew," Rick told him.

"Well," John said, slapping him on the shoulder, "while you're thinking, why don't you ride out with me to check the herd. Get your mind on something else. Maybe the answer will come to you when you're not trying so hard to find it."

Rick grinned. "This just an excuse to get me back in a saddle?"

"Damn straight. Want to see if all that walking you do as a marine has made you forget how to ride a horse."

"That'll be the day," Rick assured him. "But Sadie and the girls are coming here for dinner, so I can't be out long."

"Then we better get moving. Unless like I said, you don't feel comfortable on a horse anymore."

"You want to see comfortable?" Rick steered the older man toward the stable. "I'll race you out to the north pasture."

"What do I get when I win?" John asked.

Rick laughed and, damn, it felt good. The summer sun was shining. Sadie and his daughters would be there soon. He was home, on land that called to his soul, and for the first time in a long time, he began to think that home was right where he belonged.

"Castle!"

"It's not a castle, sweetie," Sadie whispered to Wendy as she set the little girl down beside her sister. Then Sadie picked up the stuffed diaper bags and looked up at Rick's ranch house.

"Is castle," Gail insisted.

"Okay," Sadie said on a sigh, surrendering to the inevitable. After all, there *was* a stone tower at one end of the huge house and that was clearly enough for two girls who enjoyed storybooks about princesses at every bedtime.

Wendy clapped her little hands and took off running. Quickly, Sadie shouted, "Wendy, *freeze*."

The little girl stopped so suddenly, she toppled over, landing on her knees and palms. Her lip curled, her eyes scrunched up and a low-pitched wail slowly built to a scream.

"Hey now!" Rick came out of the house and sprinted across the lawn toward his fallen daughter. Before Sadie and Gail had taken more than a few steps forward, he had the little girl swept into his arms and was soothing her out of her tears.

"You okay, sweet thing?" Rick asked, wiping away tears with his thumb.

"Falled down," Wendy said and dropped her head onto his shoulder with a dramatic slump.

"I know, baby girl," he soothed, running one hand up and down her narrow back while his gaze searched for and found Sadie's. "But you okay now?"

"Okay," she said, lifting her head then patting his cheek. "Down," she ordered.

As he set one daughter down, Gail held her arms up to him. "Up."

"Tag teaming me?" he asked with a smile as he lifted the little girl.

"Welcome to my world," Sadie told him ruefully.

How could a man look *that* sexy while holding a child? Sadie's body was humming, her blood simmering and the low, deep-down ache she'd been carrying around for days began to pulse in time with her heartbeat.

"Happy to be here." His voice was low, a soft touch on her already ragged nerve endings.

Honestly, after being around him so much for the last week, Sadie was in sad, sad shape. Oh, she still wouldn't consider marrying a man who only wanted her because she had given birth to his children. But she wasn't above admitting just how badly she wanted him.

And that was a dangerous feeling.

He was a marine. Trained to spot his opponent's weakness. She sighed to herself. Judging by the wicked gleam in his eye, he was doing just that.

"I'm glad you came," he said after a long moment filled only with the twins' excited jabbering.

Those eyes of his were really lethal weapons, she thought. So dark. So deep. Filled with old pains and secrets, so much so that any woman would be tempted to get closer. To discover the man within. To do just what she had done three years ago, Sadie reminded herself sternly.

She remembered it all so clearly, it could have happened the day before. Sadie had been at Claire's restaurant, trying to look as though she didn't mind eating alone. Rick had walked in, strolled over to her table and asked if he could join her.

She had been so lonely, so…lost, that she had said yes. For once in her oh-so-proper life, Sadie dropped her shields, lowered her guard and had allowed the *real* her to come storming out to play. She had held nothing back that night and, in return, she had experienced real passion. Real fire.

They shared dinner, then a walk around the lake, then a drive to a hotel in Midland, then hours of amazing sex. And over the course of that incredible night, Rick had taught Sadie that her ex-husband had been wrong when he accused her of being a frigid ice queen.

Memories rushed through her mind with a staggering force that left Sadie breathless. Image after image rose up within her, bringing back every second of that long-ago night until Sadie practically vibrated with need.

She dragged air into her lungs and forced herself to keep her gaze locked with his. She had succumbed to those eyes and that mouth once. She wasn't going to do it again. She was stronger than her need.

"The girls have been looking forward to coming," she said, stroking one hand across Wendy's soft curls.

Thank God she had the twins with her, she thought. They would be her safety net. She and Rick couldn't very well indulge in hot, steamy, wonderful, frenzied sex with their daughters in attendance, now could they?

Oh, yeah, she thought. *Sad, sad, shape.*

"Not you though, huh?"

"This isn't about me," Sadie told him, even while her mind was taunting, *liar, liar.* Of course she had been looking forward to seeing him. He was all she thought about lately. The man filled her mind while she was awake and starred in her dreams when she managed to sleep.

"Babe, it's *all* about you."

She stiffened. "I told you once, don't—"

"—call you baby." He grinned. "I didn't. Called you babe."

"That's the same thing," she told him, but couldn't quite seem to keep her lips from twitching.

No other man she had ever known had teased her, flirted with her, treated her like…a woman. Most men around here were so deferential, all they saw was the Price name, never Sadie herself.

"How about *darlin'* then?" he asked, deliberately drawing out the word until it became a deep, Southern caress.

"How about we stick with Sadie?"

He shrugged and smiled again. "That'll do. For now."

She took a breath, hoping to steady herself. Instead, she got a whiff of freshly showered male and felt her ragged nerve endings fray just a little bit more.

"How about we go inside?" That delectable smile of his curved his mouth in invitation. "I want to show the girls their room."

He was already headed for the house, Gail on his hip, Wendy's hand tucked into his when his words finally settled in Sadie's mind.

"Their *room?*"

"Cozy as two kittens, aren't they?" he asked, fifteen minutes later, his gaze never leaving the two little girls.

"Why wouldn't they be?" Sadie shook her head as she looked around the pink-and-white splendor.

Twin youth beds, guardrails in place, were covered by lacy white quilts with pink scrolling spelling out each girl's name in flowing script. White dressers stood alongside each girl's bed and a collection of stuffed animals sat perched on little-girl-size rocking chairs. Pink curtains hung at the wide windows that were also gated for safety. There were matching toy boxes, two rocking horses and two identical castle playhouses, complete with tiny dolls and furniture.

The walls were white, with a mural of spring flowers sprouting up from the gleaming wood floor. A rose-colored braided rug in the center of the room provided warmth and comfort. As if even Heaven approved of what Rick had done here, sunlight speared into the room, dazzling it all with a golden glow.

He had only known about the twins' existence for two weeks and yet he'd managed to create a little girl's paradise. She should be pleased, she knew. Instead, a pang of worry reverberated inside her. This was permanence. Rick was making an important statement here. Letting not only his daughters but Sadie know that he was going to be a part of their lives from here on out.

"You like it?" he asked, shattering her thoughts and dragging her gaze back to his.

"What's not to like?" Sadie walked farther into the room and watched her girls delightedly exploring. "How did you get all of this done so quickly?"

"Amazing what enough money in the right hands can accomplish." He leaned against the doorjamb, folded his arms across his chest and narrowed his eyes on her.

A flicker of heat skittered through her system under that watchful stare. "Why?" she asked. "Why do this if you're leaving again? By the time you get back, they'll be too old for this room."

He frowned and his eyes darkened. "I haven't decided yet what I'm going to do, but whatever it is, the girls will be a part of my life. I wanted them to have a place here. To know this ranch as home."

"Their home is with me," Sadie said quietly with a quick glance at the girls as they squabbled over the stuffed animals.

"Could be with both of us," he pointed out.

"Don't start again, Rick," she said with a shake of her head. "We've been down that road too many times already."

"And never really talked about it."

"There's nothing to say."

When the girls scampered into an adjoining room, Sadie grabbed at the excuse to halt her conversation with Rick and called out, "Hold on, you two...."

"Don't worry," Rick said quickly, reaching out to take her hand. At the first touch of his skin to hers, Sadie sucked in a gulp of air. She felt his reaction as strongly as her own and she knew that whatever else lay between them, the sexual heat was still burning fiercely.

He gave her hand a squeeze and released her reluctantly. "Nothing in here can hurt them. I had experts come in and baby-proof the place. Hell, the whole house has had a toddler remodel."

Sadie curled her fingers into a fist to keep from reaching out to him again just to feel that sizzle of heat. Nodding to him, she relaxed her guard on the girls a little.

She'd already noticed the window gates and the plugs in the electrical outlets. And she had to admit that, even with the worry over Rick trying to swoop her girls out from under her, she was touched that he'd gone to so much trouble. But still... "What's in that room?"

He tucked his hands into his jeans pockets and shrugged. "Not a room. It's their closet."

"Their—" Stunned speechless, she followed her girls and found them pawing through rack after rack of dresses, shirts and jeans. The closet had been designed so that everything was on toddler level, so both girls had no trouble reaching all of the new clothing that had been purchased just for them.

On the floor of the closet, clear boxes of different types of shoes were stacked. Chortling gleefully, the twins indulged themselves. Wendy was tugging at a pair of miniature cowboy boots, while Gail was trying to force her sneaker-clad foot into a princess slipper.

"Sweetie, wait a minute," Sadie said, dropping to her knees and taking the slipper from greedy little hands.

"Wanna," Gail argued, her bottom lip poking out in a pout that was a herald of a tantrum to come.

Sadie braced for it, almost looking forward to seeing Rick handle one of his daughters when she was less than the loveable toddler he knew. But she didn't get a chance. Instead, she listened.

"Well, now, you two girls could play in here…or we could go and see your ponies," he coaxed.

"Pony!" Both of them leaped up and charged to Rick as if he was Santa Claus. And no doubt that's just what he looked like to two dazzled little girls.

Their mother however, was a different story. "Ponies?"

"Tiny ones," Rick assured her, scooping both girls up into his arms. "Really. Hardly even related to horses, they're so small."

"The girls don't need ponies," Sadie said, congratulating herself on the calm even tone of her voice.

He grinned. "Wouldn't be much fun to get things only when you *need* them, would it?"

"Pony, Mommy!" Wendy slapped her hands together and Gail laid her head down on her father's shoulder.

Sadie, looking at the three of them united together against her, knew she'd lost this battle. Rick was making all of her girls' dreams come true. From the castlelike tower on his house, to princess shoes, to ponies. Heaven knew what would be next. Just that thought was enough to have her say quietly, "Rick, you can't keep doing this. You'll spoil them rotten."

Surprise etched itself into his features. "How can you spoil a child by loving her?"

She sighed again. The man was hopeless.

"Sadie, I missed their first two years." He looked from one tiny face to the other. "I missed too much. Let me make it up to them *and* to myself."

She looked at the three of them and something inside her liquefied, becoming a warm, bubbling pool of emotion. How was she supposed to stand firm when he melted her with his love for their girls?

Shaking her head, she said, "I draw the line at them *riding* those ponies. At least not until they're three."

"Riding alone? Absolutely not. But we can hold them in the saddles..." he coaxed.

"You're impossible."

"To resist, you mean," he added with a wink.

"Watch me," she countered.

"I do," he said softly. "Every chance I get."

John Henry's wife Elena had made them dinner. A feast of enchiladas, rice and homemade beans. The twins had their supper upstairs, with the older woman who had insisted on taking care of them to give Rick and Sadie time to talk.

Rick made a mental note to give Elena a raise. He'd been wanting to get Sadie all to himself for hours. God knows, he loved those two girls, but their mother was his main focus. With dinner over, dishes done, he had a chance to simply sit with her in the moonlight.

For two weeks now, he'd spent nearly every day with Sadie and their daughters. And while he was enjoying getting to know his girls, what he craved was getting reacquainted with Sadie. She was making him crazy.

Dinner on the stone patio, with candles in hurricane lamps and music drifting to them from inside the house was as romantic a setting as he could imagine. Having the woman driving him to distraction sitting across from him was just the icing on the proverbial cake.

"That was wonderful," Sadie said, sipping at her wine.

"Elena's the best cook in Texas."

Above them, the moon rose in the sky and a soft wind rattled the leaves of the black oaks standing along the perimeter of the yard. The candle on the table dipped and swayed behind its glass walls and the resulting shadows played across Sadie's features.

"I've thought about you," he said quietly. "A lot over the last few years."

She dipped her head then looked up at him from beneath lowered lashes. "I thought about you a lot, too."

He grinned. "Yeah, I can imagine you did, what with those two little reminders running around."

"It wasn't just the girls," she admitted.

"Glad to hear that," he said, and his pulse quickened. Getting Sadie to acknowledge that there was something between them was just the first step. He had to remind her how good they had been together. Had to show her what they could have together now.

She smiled to herself and lifted her face to the night sky. "It doesn't change anything, Rick. Wanting you, I mean."

"From where I'm sitting it does."

"Excuse me." Elena stepped out onto the patio. "I hate interrupting, but I wanted to let you know, both girls are fast asleep."

"Asleep?" Sadie sat up straighter. "I should just take them home."

"Let them stay," Rick said quietly.

"Honestly, Miss Price," Elena told her, "the two of them were just worn out with excitement. I gave them a bath, put them in their pajamas and tucked them right in. They're just fine. The monitor's been turned on and I brought one of the receivers out here for you to keep tabs on them."

She set the white receiver down onto the table and Sadie looked at it. Rick knew she was thinking about just packing up the girls and running for the hills, but damned if he'd let her. This was working out great. He hadn't planned for the girls to fall asleep, but now that they had, he wouldn't waste his alone time with their mother.

"You two enjoy your evening," Elena said. "I'm just heading home myself." She walked across the patio, slipped through the line of trees and disappeared into the shadows, headed for the Henry house just beyond the stable.

"I didn't plan for the girls to stay here with you tonight." She reached for the monitor and turned up the volume.

"You could all stay," he said, getting up to walk to her side of the table.

"Oh, that's not a good idea," she said, even as he pulled her to her feet.

"Best idea I've heard in three years," Rick argued. He smoothed his hands through her long, blond hair and then cupped her face in his palms.

She shivered and a tiny sigh erupted from her throat. "Rick…"

"Stop thinking, Sadie," he whispered and bent to kiss her briefly, sweetly. "Just for tonight, stop thinking."

"We did that once, remember?" She was arguing, but her hands settled at his waist and he felt the heat of her soaking inside him.

"Yeah. I remember. All of it. The feel of you, the taste

of you." He kissed her again, teasing the part in her lips with the tip of his tongue. Every inch of his body was on fire for her. The last couple of weeks, being close to her and yet so damned separate, had been torture. "Do you know, for months after I deployed, I could close my eyes and smell you on me?"

"Oh, my…"

He bent to kiss the curve of her neck and Sadie swayed into him. Breathing deep, Rick groaned in satisfaction. "There it is," he said, his breath moving over her skin, "that scent that is purely you. Smells like summer. Smells like Heaven."

"Rick, you're not playing fair…."

"I know," he said, smiling against her skin, then nibbling at the elegant line of her throat until she shivered again. "I don't want to be fair, Sadie. I want *you*."

"*Really* not fair," she murmured, hands sweeping up to splay against his back and hold him closer. "But you know this wouldn't solve anything."

"Not asking it to," he whispered.

"It would probably only make things harder."

"Things are pretty hard right now," he confessed, lifting his head to smile down at her.

She laughed and shook her head. "How am I supposed to fight you?"

"You're not. I'm tired of fighting, Sadie. And so are you." He kissed her then, long and deep, tongue tangling with hers, silently demanding that she feel what he felt, want what he wanted.

Finally, though, he broke the kiss, lifted his head and looked into her eyes. He read passion glittering there and knew he'd won this round. Knew that her needs were going to overpower her sense of propriety. Just as they had that night three years ago.

He dropped his hands to her waist, then skimmed his palms up, beneath the hem of her yellow silk shirt. Her skin was softer than that silk and just touching her again inflamed him more than he had expected. His body went rock-hard and aching. His heartbeat pounded in his chest and need clamped a tight fist around his lungs so that breathing was nearly impossible.

Her eyes locked with his and when he covered her breasts with his hands, he saw the flare of desire quickening in those pale blue depths. Even through the lace of her bra, he felt her nipples pebble at his caress. Felt the sweeping rush of heat that was going to engulf them both.

"I am tired of fighting you. Fighting *this*," she said, arching into him, silently asking for more. "So touch me again. Touch me all over. Make me feel the way you did on that night."

He wouldn't have thought it possible to get even harder, but he did. Hearing her ask for him. Seeing her desire. Feeling her heat.

Rick was lost.

Right where he wanted to be.

Seven

With the summer wind blowing all around them like a soft caress, Sadie forgot about standing her ground and gave herself up to the wonder of being in Rick's arms again.

Her entire life, she had done the right thing, said the right thing, been the perfect daughter. Yes, she'd gotten a divorce, but even society expected that to happen once in a while. Until that night with Rick, she had never really rebelled. And in that one night, she had felt more alive than she ever had before.

She wanted it again.

His kiss enveloped her. Their tongues danced in a sensual feast of sensation until Sadie was panting for air and not really caring if she got her next breath or not. Her hands swept up and down his back, loving the feel of his hard, muscled body pressed against her.

He grabbed her and pulled her abdomen close enough

that she felt the thick heaviness of his body. Desire pumped through them both with a rush that was simply shattering. There were so many sensations. So many emotions churning inside her.

Rick unbuttoned her blouse and slid it off her shoulders and down her arms to puddle on the stone patio at their feet. She lifted her arms to him, encircled his neck and gloried in the feel of his hands moving over her bare flesh. In moments, he had unhooked her bra and dropped it, too, to the patio.

Then he set her back from him and looked his fill. The warm summer air felt cool on her heated skin. He bent his head and took first one hardened nipple then the other into his mouth. His lips, tongue and teeth tortured her gently, sending her mind spinning out of control as her instincts took over.

She groaned and held his head to her breast, smoothing her fingers through his short hair, loving the slide of it against her skin. He suckled her and she felt everything inside her liquefy in a rush of molten heat that settled deep at her core.

"Rick…" She swayed into him as her knees went weak in response to the overload of sensation. "I'm going to fall over here in a minute."

"I'm going to lay you down in a minute."

A stirring of unease mixed with excitement lit up her insides. "Out here?"

"We're alone, honey," he said, kissing her again, lightly, teasingly. "There's not a soul around."

"But Elena. John Henry—"

"Never leave their place at night. No more buts, darlin'," he told her, laying one finger across her lips to keep her protests quiet. "Just relax and trust me. Can you do that?"

She looked up into his eyes and realized that she had already made her decision. She wanted another night with Rick. He was the man who had shown her what real passion and excitement was. Did she really want to back away now?

"I can do that," she said before her rational mind could override her desires.

"Just what I wanted to hear," he said and tore off his own shirt.

She reached for him, unable to keep from stroking her fingertips along that bronzed, sculpted chest. He sucked in some air at her touch and Sadie smiled to know that she was having the same kind of effect on him that he was on her.

A purely female, sexual power swirled through her as she ran her palms across his flat nipples and when his eyes narrowed and his jaw clenched, she loved the rush she felt.

"Sadie, you are making me crazy."

"That's the nicest thing you've ever said to me," she said huskily, leaning in to kiss him.

He chuckled and the sound was dark and rich, rolling through her system like warm wine.

"This is crazy," she murmured, knowing it was true, but not really caring. "Heck, *you're* crazy," she added and even she thought it sounded more like a compliment than an accusation.

"It's part of what you like about me," he said and led her to the double-wide chaise. It was warm from the summer sun and overstuffed to make lounging on the patio as comfortable as possible. And Sadie could hardly believe that she was stripping out of her clothes and lying down on it, naked in the moonlight.

The heavy cotton felt scratchy against her skin, but

any discomfort was lost as she watched Rick quickly get rid of his clothes. She sucked in a gulp of air when she took her first look at his body, hard and ready for her. Then she couldn't think at all because he was there, lying on top of her, flesh to flesh, heat to heat.

She sighed when he rolled to his back and pulled her on top of him. She straddled him then, looking down into dark eyes that flashed with wicked heat. He lifted both hands to cup her bare breasts and at the first touch of his hands, she arched into him, pushing herself into his grasp. Sighing, she let all thought slide away as his fingers and thumbs tweaked at her already sensitive nipples.

She needed to touch as well as be touched. Reaching down, she wrapped her hands around his heavy shaft and smiled when he hissed in a breath through gritted teeth. She stroked him, rubbing her fingers up and down his length and across the very tip of him until he was lifting his hips into her touch.

"You're killing me," he groaned.

"Oh, not my intention at all," Sadie promised. Then, feeling sexy and wild and completely out of control, she went up on her knees and slowly, slowly took him into her body. Inch by glorious inch, she accepted him, giving her own body time to stretch to accommodate his. It was an invasion of the most intimate kind and she wanted all of him within her.

She took her time, prolonging the suspenseful glide of bodies locking together to torture both of them. Her eyes closed and she moaned her pleasure.

"Enough," he grumbled a moment later and rolled them over again, until Sadie was on her back and he was wedged between her thighs.

She smiled up at him. "Impatient."

"Damn right. We've waited three years to do this. So let's get to it."

"You are a romantic, aren't you, Rick Pruitt?"

"Darlin', you, naked, in the moonlight—that's as romantic as it gets."

"Smooth talker." She wrapped her arms around his neck and lifted her hips to him.

He pushed deeper inside her and Sadie gasped, tipping her head back to look up at the stars. He was inside her. Filling her. And for the first time in three years, she felt…complete.

He moved then, rocking his hips, setting a rhythm that she raced to match. Her gaze fixed on his, as if his dark brown eyes held every secret she had ever wanted to know. Breath laboring, bodies straining together, they held on to each other and hurtled toward the explosive release waiting for them.

Rick bent his head to take her mouth with his as the first of the tremors wracked her body. She tasted him as a shattering climax claimed her. Sadie held him tightly, shuddering as ripple after ripple of pleasure roared through her.

And before the last of those tremors died away, he groaned and, still kissing her desperately, emptied all that he was into her depths.

Two hours and lots of sex later, they were lying in Rick's bed, just down the hall from their sleeping daughters. The monitor was on the dresser, their clothes were in a heap on the floor and their heartbeats were just beginning to slow down to normal.

Curled up beside him, Sadie rested her head on Rick's chest and took a long, shaky breath. She hadn't felt this good in years. But she knew there would be a price to pay for it. Sleeping with him was going to reopen the talk of marriage and she had the feeling he wasn't going to like hearing her say no again.

"It's good," he said softly, going up on one elbow to look down at her. "Having you here in my bed. Having our daughters sleeping just down the hall."

Sadie sighed. "Rick, what we did tonight doesn't change anything for me."

He smoothed her hair back from her face and she closed her eyes briefly to enjoy the gentle caress. "It changes everything, darlin'."

"No." Opening her eyes, she swallowed back her own needs and fought to remain logical. "It's not me you really want, Rick—"

"Oh, I think the last couple of hours should have convinced you you're wrong about that."

She had to chuckle at that, since her body was still buzzing from his careful attention to detail. "I *mean,* what you want is family. You just found out about the girls and you want them in your life, I understand that. But this isn't about *me.*"

He took a breath and blew it out before saying quietly, "The first time I saw you, you were about seven years old, I think."

"What?"

"My parents took me to dinner at Claire's restaurant and I saw you at another table with Brad and your folks.…"

She scooted out from under his touch and braced her back against the headboard. "I don't see what any of this has to do with—"

"I remember," he continued as if she hadn't spoken, "because I was ten years old and didn't much like girls. But then I saw you. Your long blond hair was pulled back by a pink headband and you were wearing a white dress with ruffles. You looked like a pretty doll sitting there with your hands folded in your lap."

A pretty doll. Funny, Sadie told herself, that was how she'd felt most of her life. Not that her parents hadn't loved her, but she had never really been allowed to be a child. She was always in a dress. Always told to sit up straight. Always expected to be perfect.

Which was why she'd made sure her daughters owned more pairs of play pants than they did dresses. At least until Rick came long.

"And I remember the waitress hurrying past your table and she spilled a Coke. It dropped onto your lap and I can still see your reaction in my mind."

"Oh, God," she whispered, "I remember that."

She hadn't thought about it in years. Now that she had though, the day came back in a rush of memories that had her cringing inside.

Rick sat up beside her, tucked a pillow behind her back and then took her hand in his. "You didn't shout or scream in surprise. You just sat there, your white, lacy lap filled with dark brown cola and you cried." His thumb moved back and forth across her hand. "Big, silent tears, while your mom rushed to clean you up and the waitress babbled apologies. Your dad didn't even look at you, he just took Brad and led him outside."

"He never did like scenes," Sadie whispered.

They were having Sunday dinner at Claire's because her father considered it good business to frequent local establishments. He always said, they were the Price family and it was up to them to set an example for others. He said that it was important that people think well of them so they were always to be on their best behavior.

When they got home that night, her father had made

a point of telling her that she had comported herself well by not throwing a hissy fit in the diner. He said it was all the waitress's fault, but that everyone in town would be talking about what a perfect lady Sadie was.

A lady.

At seven.

It had been a stifling way to grow up, Sadie thought now.

"You were still a beauty at sixteen," he said, leaning down now to plant a kiss on her forehead.

Relieved to have a change of subject, Sadie laughed. "Oh, please. You never knew I was alive when we were teenagers."

"That right?" He dropped one arm around her shoulders and pulled her in close to him. "I was playing basketball with some guys one day at the park when you walked by with Abby and a couple of other girls. Don't remember who they were, because my memory's all about you. Your hair was long and you had it pulled back into a ponytail. You were wearing white pants and a red top and you were smiling at something. And I thought you were the most beautiful thing I'd ever seen."

"You're making that up."

"I called your name and threw the basketball to you. You were surprised, but you caught it. Then you looked at me like you didn't have a clue what to do next and you just set the damn thing down on the grass and walked away."

Her heart softened at his words as she realized that he had noticed her all those years ago. And she wondered what might have happened between them if she'd had enough courage back then to actually talk to him.

"Oh, God, I remember that, too." She laughed a little uneasily. "I didn't know what to do. I wanted to throw it back to you, but I was afraid I'd do it wrong and look foolish in front of everyone. So I didn't do it at all. It's the Price way," she told him softly. "Always worry about what people will think."

"Doesn't matter," he said, "wasn't my point."

"What is the point then, Rick?" Yes, knowing that he noticed her was lovely, but talking about the past didn't change the future.

"You were always the unattainable, beautiful Sadie Price," he told her.

"I was," she said softly, shaking her head at the swarm of memories his words had created. "My parents put me on a shelf and kept me there until I was old enough to marry the 'right' man. Of course, he turned out to be all wrong."

"Maybe," he answered, "what you need to do is marry the 'wrong' man who might turn out to be just right."

She looked at him. "You just don't give up, do you?"

"I'm a marine, darlin'. We never surrender."

"God, why are you so stubborn?"

"When I see something I want, I go get it."

"Why me?"

"Hell, have you *seen* you? You're beautiful. Smart. Sexy as hell. And, oh, yeah. The mother of my children."

"There it is again," she said, pushing out of his arms. Sliding to the edge of the bed, she got up and walked to the window overlooking the front yard. Then she turned and speared him with a hard look. "That's the real reason for your pursuit. For your proposals."

"What's wrong with that?"

"I don't want to be the next duty you pick up and shoulder because you think it's the right thing to do. I want to be wanted for *me*."

Now he pushed off the bed and stalked to her side. "I just proved to you that I do want you."

"Rick, we're arguing in circles," Sadie said, laying both hands on his bare chest. "We don't agree. We're not going to agree. So can we just at least drop it?"

He sighed, then pulled her to him, wrapping his arms around her and holding her close. "We can do that. I don't want to waste what we've got fighting over what we don't. So yeah, we can drop it. For now."

She closed her eyes as she laid her head on his chest. That wasn't a concession, she knew. Rick wasn't the kind of man who would give up and walk away from what he perceived as his duty.

But for tonight at least, there was a ceasefire.

A few days later, Sadie was sitting in the TCC dining room having lunch with Abby. The girls were with Hannah, and Sadie hadn't seen Rick since their amazing night together.

She was torn between relief and fury. She should be happy he was backing off as she had asked him to. On the other hand, for a guy who said he never gave up, he was giving up awfully easily.

"You look serious," Abby commented, lifting her glass of iced tea for a sip. "Or is that furious?"

"A little of both, I guess," Sadie admitted. She gave a quick look around.

The dining room was crowded, as it always was at lunchtime. There were members and their wives, seated at the elegant tables. Whispers of conversation rose and fell like the tide and the smooth wait staff moved in and out of the crowd in a seamless dance that was practically choreographed.

Lowering her voice, Sadie said, "It's Rick, of course."

"Naturally. How're things going with him, anyway? Haven't talked to you since the Fourth."

A flush swept up Sadie's cheeks and she was glad that the lighting in the TCC was so dim. Otherwise, everyone in the room would have seen her pale skin burning red. Bad enough that Abby was close enough to notice.

"Well, that's intriguing," Abby said, flipping her long, dark red hair back over her shoulder. Then she narrowed sharp blue eyes and ordered, "Tell me everything."

Sadie did. Leaving out the details of that sinfully sexy night, she got right down to the bare bones of it.

"Chemistry, oh, yes," she said as she was winding down, "we've got that, there's no doubt. But, Abby, he keeps insisting he wants to marry me despite me telling him no at every turn."

"And why is it again you're turning him down?"

Sadie looked at her friend in stunned surprise. "Because he's only asking because of the girls."

Abby smirked and took a sip of tea. She shook her head. "Doesn't sound like it to me. Sounds like he's asking because he can't keep his hands off of you."

A stir of something hot and wicked whipped through Sadie at the words. But she wouldn't be fooled by her own passions. "No. This is about duty. Plain and simple."

Their waiter appeared to deliver two enormous Cobb salads and when he was gone again, Sadie changed the subject. "I'm so tired of thinking and talking about me. What's going on with you and Brad?"

Abby snorted and picked up her fork to stab a slice of hard-boiled egg. "Firstly there *is* no me and Brad. There is simply me battering away at your thick-as-a-post brother."

"And good luck with that," Sadie told her. "But what's happening with the club?"

Abby looked around now, checking to make sure no one was listening. "Brad is running for president of the club and judging from what I've heard, he's pretty much got the position sewn up."

"Uh-oh," Sadie said, thinking that this couldn't possibly end well.

"Exactly. If Brad wins the presidency, then he'll find a way to not only get rid of me, but to keep all women out of the club forever."

"Sounds like him," Sadie admitted.

"Absolutely it does," Abby told her, dropping her fork with a clatter against the ceramic bowl. "*And* the man will find a way to keep this club locked into the past. Honestly, he is infuriating. He's so hidebound to tradition, he should be living in the nineteenth century."

"Also sounds like him," Sadie concurred.

"Well, he's not going to best me," Abby vowed. "You know, all of this started with the talk of rebuilding the club—which I still think is a great idea."

"I can sort of see Brad's point," Sadie said as she looked around the familiar room. Her father was a member of the club and his family was welcome in the public dining room. She had been going there all her life for special occasions. In a way, the thought of it changing sent a pang through her.

"Are you serious?" Abby asked, dumbfounded. "I mean, yes, tradition is nice, but so is central heating!"

Sadie held up one hand, palm out. "I'm with you. Honest. On your side."

"Glad to hear it. For a second there, I was worried that you were slipping over to the enemy team." Ruefully, Abby smiled and took a breath. "Right. Sorry. I get a little steamed when I start talking about Brad."

"Did you ever notice that it's always *men* making

women insane?" Sadie took a sip of her tea and pushed chopped ham around on top of the bed of lettuce in front of her. She didn't really have an appetite, which she also blamed on Rick.

Why wasn't he getting in touch with her?

Was sex all he had wanted?

Were all of his proposals meaningless?

And *why* did she care? This was what she wanted, right?

She groaned and Abby reached over to pat her shoulder in support. "Of course it's men who make us crazy. Women understand each other. It's the Y chromosome that makes everything so irritating."

"So, have you decided what you're going to do about your irritation?"

"Not yet," Abby admitted, but her eyes took on a calculating gleam. "I do have a few ideas, though. It's time we finally break through and tear down the last of the old boy's club barriers around here."

Sadie laughed and felt a little easier. Sure, her situation with Rick was up in the air and more confusing than ever. But at least she wasn't alone in her confusion.

Before she could so much as start in on her salad again, Sadie sensed a subtle shift in the club's atmosphere. The conversations around them were still going on, but there was more of a hush to them now. As if everyone was suddenly interested in the same thing.

"Oh, my," Abby whispered and tapped Sadie's hand.

When she looked up, she turned her gaze to where Abby was pointing and Sadie actually *felt* her stomach drop. Rick was standing in the entryway, dressed in his uniform, an expression of steely determination carved into his face.

In spite of everything, Sadie's stomach did a quick

lurch and spin as adrenaline-spiked excitement dropped into the pit of her belly. She hadn't seen him in days. And now that he was here, right in front of her, her body was lighting up like a Christmas tree.

Darn it.

His gaze locked with hers, Rick strode across the crowded dining room like a man on a mission. As he came closer and closer, Sadie's heart began to pound in anticipation, even as she fought to keep her emotions off her face.

The crowd around them seemed to sense that something special was up. Conversations dwindled away, and as Rick crossed the room, even the wait staff froze in place. It was like the whole room had taken a breath and held it.

He stopped beside their table and spared a quick look at Abby. "Nice to see you," he said.

"You, too," Abby murmured, her gaze shifting to Sadie.

"Sadie," Rick announced, his voice easily carrying across the crowd. "I've got something to say to you."

"Oh God," she mumbled, trying not to notice the dozens of curious stares directed at her.

"And I don't care if the whole world hears me," Rick continued. "Hell, I want them to hear me."

"Don't do this," Sadie whispered, her eyes on him.

"I have to," Rick said.

He'd finally figured out that the one sure way to get Sadie to agree to marry him was to ask her in front of people. The way she was raised, the woman she was, wouldn't allow her to embarrass either him or herself by refusing him.

So he'd spent the last few days finding the perfect ring and waiting for his best opportunity. When he'd discovered she was going to be here at the club having lunch with Abby, Rick made his move.

She was stunned. He could see it on her face, despite how hard she was trying to hide it. Just like that time when she was a girl in the diner, she wouldn't let anyone know what she was feeling or thinking. She would be a lady and do the only thing she could do.

She would finally say yes.

Keeping his gaze locked with hers, he made an elaborate show of dropping to one knee. Then he opened up the small, navy-blue jeweler's box and showed her the enormous diamond he'd picked out for her, making sure the rest of the crowd got a good look, too.

Their audience took a breath and the sound was audible. Sadie just blinked at him. When he had everyone's attention, he spoke, in a loud, clear voice, "Sadie Price, will you marry me? Will you let me be a father to our children?"

Then he waited for her quiet acceptance.

Eight

"You son of a—" Sadie bit off the last word, but no one in the room had any doubt of what she meant.

Rick slowly stood up and watched as glints of raw, gut-deep anger erupted in her usually placid blue eyes. Okay, maybe he might have made a tactical error here.

Abby was chuckling, covering her mouth with one hand to hide her smile. The rest of the room was blistering with questions and comments. He only caught a handful.

"What'll she say?"

"That's Sadie Price. She'll do the right thing."

"If I was her, I'd slap him for embarrassing me like that."

"Well," another woman mused aloud, "if she doesn't want him, I'll take him."

He didn't care what any of them had to say. The only opinion he was interested in was Sadie's. And it didn't look to him that he was going to get the answer he wanted.

Rick scowled as Sadie pushed herself out of the maroon leather booth seat, grabbed her purse and flung a look back at Abby. "Thanks for lunch but I have to go now."

"I can see that. I'll call you later."

She jerked a fast nod, then fired another look at Rick. "*You,* I want to talk to. *Outside.*"

Then she marched across the crowded dining room like a young queen. People's heads turned to watch her pass and a few of the men shot Rick sympathetic glances.

He wasn't interested in sympathy. Snapping the ring box closed, he stuffed it into his pocket and followed his woman out of the club.

The door hardly had a chance to swing shut behind them when she turned on him like a snake.

"What were you *thinking?*"

The summer sun hammered them both the minute they stepped outside. It was like trying to draw a breath through a wet electric blanket. But the vicious heat had nothing on the fury stamped on Sadie's face.

Gritting his teeth, Rick scrubbed one hand across his face. "I was thinking that I want to marry you. Just like I've been thinking for more than two weeks now."

She threw her hands high then let them fall to her sides again in complete exasperation. "And the fact that I've turned you down countless times didn't enter your head?"

"No," he snapped, irritated as all hell that his plan had fallen so flat. He would have bet cold, hard cash on Sadie Price coming down on the side of decorum. It had never occurred to him that she might not leap into his arms for the sake of the watching crowds.

He could see now, it should have.

"I can't believe you did that in front of half the town."

"Seemed like a good idea at the time," he muttered and flashed a glare at a man who stopped to stare at them. Quickly, the bystander hurried on down the sidewalk.

"And I can guess why," she said, stepping close enough that she could poke her index finger into his chest. "Now that the word's out around town and everyone knows that you're the girls' father, you figured they'd all be on your side. And you thought that I'd say yes to avoid making a scene."

His mouth worked as he fought to keep back the words that would damn him.

"You're a worm for trying to use that against me."

"Darlin', I'm gonna use every weapon I've got when I'm facing down a hardheaded opponent."

"I am *not* hardheaded just because I don't want the same thing you do."

"You are if you refuse to see sense just to prove a point."

She sucked in a gulp of air and stared at him as if he'd just sprouted two heads. "Do you really think I'm that small and petty?" she demanded.

A couple of people strolled past, caught a whiff of their argument and picked up speed.

"I didn't say that," Rick told her.

"You might as well have."

"Don't put words in my mouth."

"Why the hell not? That's exactly what you were trying to do to me." She glared at him with a fire that should have scorched him.

"All I did was ask you a question!"

"In public! Was that your idea of a romantic proposal?"

"I *tried* romance, Sadie!" He loomed over her, but to give her due, she didn't back down an inch. "I had you naked in the moonlight, remember?"

"Well, I never heard such a thing!" An older woman stopped dead as she passed them and slanted Rick a horrified look.

"Mrs. Mulaney," Sadie muttered, never taking her gaze from Rick's.

The older woman gave Rick the evil eye. "You should be ashamed of yourself, Rick Pruitt," she snapped. "Sadie, dear, do you need me to call a policeman?"

"No, ma'am, thank you."

"We're fine, thanks," Rick told the older woman with the iron-gray hair and the sucked-on-a-lemon expression. Mrs. Mulaney was the town librarian and lived her life as though it were her duty to tell people "hush" everywhere in town.

"I wasn't speaking to you, Rick Pruitt! But I should think a United States Marine would know better how to conduct himself." She hurried on as if dogs were chasing her.

"That's just perfect," Sadie muttered. "Now Mrs. Mulaney knows that I was naked in the moonlight with you. Just great. That should take about ten minutes to get all over town."

He smirked at her, knowing he'd just scored a point. "Thought you don't care what anyone thinks about you anymore."

"I don't," she snapped. "Not enough to say yes to a marriage proposal that I know you don't even really want to make."

"You *are* crazy," he countered. "I've been straight up with you, Sadie, right from the beginning. I told you I want to marry you. Be a daddy to our daughters. *You're* the one holding back here."

She took a deep breath, held it for a second and then let it slide from her lungs as she shook her head.

"You know," she finally said, "I should thank you. Only a few years ago, I might have accepted that proposal just to keep from making a scene in the restaurant. But because of *you,* I've found myself."

"What're you talking about?" Rick had the distinct feeling he wasn't going to like this, but he had to hear her out. How else could he plan his next move?

"I moved to Houston when I was pregnant because I didn't want to hear the talk. Didn't want the girls to hear it."

"I know that already."

"But what you don't know is, I'm not that woman anymore." Sadie looked up at him. "I've grown up at last and I like who I am now. These last couple of weeks with you have helped me there, too. I'm not perfect little Sadie Price anymore. I don't *care* what this town has to say about me or you for that matter. Let Mrs. Mulaney spill her guts. I'll hold my head up anyway. And later on, if someone's mean to my girls, I'll handle it, but I'll see to it that Wendy and Gail don't care about gossip, either."

She leaned in until their gazes locked in a silent battle of wills. "I'm going to show them so much love, so much complete acceptance for whoever they are, that *they* won't care what anyone else thinks."

There was that pride in her again. It was good to see her so sure of herself. The only downside was, she seemed to have convinced herself she didn't need *him*. And that he couldn't have.

"Sounds good to me, Sadie," he told her, reaching for her only to have her step back, evading his touch. "All of it sounds just right."

"But you don't believe it. You still think I can be maneuvered into agreeing to marry you."

A stab of shame dug into his chest and Rick didn't like the feel of it. Yes, he had tried to trick her into saying yes. So what did that say about him? That he was a desperate man, that's what.

Damned if he'd apologize for it, either. She's the one who was being unreasonable.

"Maybe I was maneuvering you…"

"Maybe?"

He sighed and felt the weight of the diamond ring in his pocket, dragging at him. This day had really not gone the way he'd planned. But there was a part of him that was standing back enjoying this moment in spite of everything.

Damn, she was magnificent. Her eyes flashing, her skin pink with temper, she was so much more than the porcelain doll her parents had made her. So much more than he had thought her to be. And he wanted her now even more than ever.

"If you're waiting to hear me say sorry," he told her with a grunt of frustration, "you've got a long wait."

"Amazing," she muttered.

"Sadie, I'm not going to keep asking you to marry me only to have you slap me down for it time and again."

"Good." She didn't look particularly happy, though.

He moved in on her, ignored the people streaming past them on the sidewalk and pushed Sadie up against the wall of the club. Hands on her shoulders, he could actually *feel* her tremble under his touch and that reaction gave him hope that all wasn't lost. Not yet, anyway.

Because as he'd warned her, he wasn't a man to give up on what he wanted. He had told her he wouldn't keep asking her to marry him and he meant it. But that didn't mean he was through *demanding* she marry him.

"I didn't get a chance to finish what I was telling you in there," he said, voice low.

"I don't want to hear it," she said and tried to pull free of his grip.

He only tightened his hold and kept her pinned to the wall, where she was so close, he felt the heat of her body radiating toward him and damned if she didn't feel hotter than the Texas sun.

"You're going to, though. This you have to hear."

"Fine." She folded her arms over her chest, cocked her head and glared up at him. "What is it?"

"You should know, I'm not reenlisting."

"What?"

He laughed shortly at the surprise in her eyes. Hell, he'd felt the same way when he'd made his decision a day or so ago. But a part of him had known from the moment he saw his daughters that he was through with the Corps. His wandering days were over and he wasn't sorry to see them go.

There was more for him right here in Royal than anything he could find elsewhere. He loved his daughters and he…cared about Sadie. He didn't love her. Wouldn't allow himself to go that far. But what they shared was important, so his decision to come back home, though not easy, had at least felt right once it was made.

"My hitch is up in two months," he was saying. "In two weeks, I've got to report back to duty, but I'll stay stateside until I'm out. Then I'm coming home. To Royal. To *you*."

"Rick," she said, clearly stunned, "I don't know what to say to you...."

"Don't have to say a thing," he whispered, leaning down until his mouth was just a breath away from hers. "I'm doing this for me as much as for you. It's time I took up the reins on the family ranch. The oil business. John Henry's getting up there in age, though God knows he wouldn't admit that. And I miss home. Have for a long time."

She reached up to cover one of his hands with hers. "This doesn't change anything, Rick."

"Everything changes, Sadie. That's all life is. A series of changes. It's up to us to recognize them when they show up."

"Not all change is for the better," she protested.

"This one is." He kissed her, leaning in until their bodies pressed together and he could feel her heartbeat thundering hard in her chest.

He parted her lips with his tongue, took her breath as his own and gave her everything he had. He poured all that he was feeling into that kiss and when it was over, he had the satisfaction of seeing her stagger unsteadily.

She opened her eyes slowly, blinking up at him as if she was waking from a dream. When their gazes met, he smiled, rubbed his thumb across her lower lip. "I'm not going anywhere, Sadie," he said softly. "I'm going to be here. For you. For our girls. And sooner or later darlin', you're going to be *mine*."

She was still dazed from that kiss, and Rick could admit silently that he felt pretty much the same way. Touching her, tasting her, always left him shaken and craving more. But that kiss would have to do both of them for a while.

"Now," Rick said, taking her arm, "I'll see you back to your table and you can finish your lunch with Abby."

Sadie shook her head. "You don't have to do that."

"Yeah, I do." He opened the door, steered her through the dining room and was completely aware of the gazes locked on him. He couldn't give a good damn. He was a man on the ragged edge of control. Sadie had pushed him about as far as he was willing to be pushed. Now it was time to take a stand.

Let her know that he wasn't going anywhere.

Ignoring everyone else in the place, Rick waited for Sadie to slide into the booth beside Abby. Then he inclined his head. "Ladies…" he said, and left.

As he walked out, he heard the whispers following him and he knew damn well what the folks were wondering.

Did she say yes? Or no?

Well, he thought grimly, let 'em wonder.

By the following afternoon, the whole damn town was speculating about Rick and Sadie. There hadn't been such a flurry of gossip since word got out that Abby Langley was a descendant of Royal's very own Texan outlaw, Jessamine Golden.

Strange how much more interesting gossip seemed when *you* weren't the subject of it.

Scowling into the sun, Rick took a pull on his cold beer and looked out over the ranch lake. He'd thought coming out here today with Joe would get his mind off Sadie, but damned if she didn't haunt him even here.

He could still taste her on his lips. Could still feel the soft, curvy pliancy of her body pressed along his. Hear the soft catch of her breath and smell that tantalizing scent that clung to her skin.

Gritting his teeth, Rick finished the beer and tossed the empty into a nearby bucket. It landed with a clatter that seemed overly loud in the stillness.

"Everybody's talking about you, you know," Joe said, swinging his pole back only to let the line and lure fly out to the center of the lake. It hit with a plunk and ripples rolled across the surface, racing toward shore.

"Yeah," Rick muttered. "I know. Good to be home, huh?"

"Well, hell, can you blame anybody? The show you put on at the TCC?" Joe shook his head. "I only wish I'd been there to see it. You could have given me a heads-up. Let me know that you were going to turn the town on its ear so I could be there to watch."

"Right. Just what I needed. One more spectator."

"People are wondering what Sadie's answer was." Joe looked at him, then snorted a laugh. "Judging from your attitude, I'm guessing she's still saying no."

"Woman won't see reason."

"What's new about that?" Joe cranked on the spinning reel, drawing his line back in so he could recast.

Rick's line lay on the water, drifting with the wind. Some fishing trip this was. He couldn't keep his mind off of Sadie long enough to bother to recast. The woman was invading every damn part of his life.

"You're not doing any of the men in town any favors, you know."

"What?" Rick determinedly picked up his pole and reeled in the line. The whirring sound was almost comforting. He was going to fish and he was going to enjoy it, damn it.

"Abby Langley had a talk with my Tina. Told her how

you're pressuring Sadie to marry you." Joe sighed and cast out again. "Now Tina's giving me grief because you're my friend."

"I'd say I'm sorry about that, but I've got my own problems." Shaking his head at the weird workings of the female mind, Rick set fresh bait on the hook.

"Yeah, well," Joe said, "from what I hear, Tina's not the only wife on the warpath, either."

"That's great." Rick shook his head and sent his newly baited hook flying. Good cast.

"Yeah, I slept on the couch last night thanks to you."

"Hey, don't blame me if Tina finally got wise and tossed your ass onto a couch."

"I'm not blaming you." Joe sighed. "My own damn fault for telling Tina I thought you were right to insist on getting married. Man, you should have heard her after I said that." He stopped and shuddered in memory. "My wife's got a temper that could make a rampaging Apache back up and rethink his options. Hell, even after all that, I still say marrying the mother of your kids is the right thing to do, everybody knows that. Now all of a sudden, that's a bad thing?"

Disgusted, Rick only muttered, "Women."

"That about says it." Joe kicked at the cooler beside him. "Hell, the only reason we've got these sandwiches to eat are because I stopped by the diner on the way over. Tina refused to make me her fried chicken. Said she wouldn't have any part in making you happy when you're making Sadie so miserable." Shaking his head, he mumbled, "Not right, cutting a man off from fried chicken with no warning."

Well, that settled it, Rick thought. Every woman in this town was as nuts as Sadie. Time was, a man who *refused* to marry the mother of his children was treated like an outcast. Now, he was getting the same treatment for *trying* to marry her.

How the hell was a man supposed to make sense of something that had zero logic behind it?

A few minutes of companionable silence passed when the only sounds were a few lazy birds halfheartedly warbling in the heat and the gentle slap of water against the shore. Sunlight glittered on the lake and glanced off it as if it were a mirror. Oaks and summer-brown hills surrounded the place and Rick took a moment to feel the familiar sense of home slide through him.

This was his life. The Corps had been good to him, no doubt. And he had been proud to serve. But his last tour in the Middle East had been a rough one. He'd lost a close friend and come damn close to losing his own life.

Hard to imagine, while standing here in the sun-washed Texas beauty, that half a world away, men and women were dying for their country. He was so accustomed now to the whine and punch of gunfire. To the roar of explosions. To the adrenaline-laced moments of kill or be killed, that coming home was going to take some getting used to.

He wanted it though.

The decision to leave the Corps was the right one for him. Destiny had taken a hand and shown him the road he should be taking and he wasn't going to turn his back on it. What he had to do now was find a way to convince Sadie that they should be walking that road together.

"So," Joe said quietly, "you're really coming home to stay?"

"Yeah." Rick nodded. "It's time. Hell, past time, probably."

Joe set the butt end of his pole down against a rock

and reached into the cooler for another couple of beers. He handed one to Rick and said quietly, "I've been meaning to talk to you about something."

"Yeah?"

"That last letter you sent me…"

Rick frowned and took a long drink. Then he stared at his beer as if looking for something to say. He didn't find anything.

"You said your friend died on a patrol."

"Yeah," Rick said and in a split instant, he was back there. Searing heat, gunfire erupting all around him, men shouting, screaming. He heard it all in his sleep. Saw it all in his dreams. He rubbed his eyes as if he could wipe away the memory, but he knew it would be with him forever.

"He saved your life, didn't he?"

"He did." Rick took a breath, stared out at the lake again because he couldn't look at Joe's friendly, concerned face and talk about what had happened to Jeff Simpson. Hell, he didn't want to talk about it at all. But he knew Joe wouldn't rest until he had the story. And, because Rick was moving back home permanently, best to get it out and done now. He steeled himself against the pain and dove in.

"It was an ambush," he said simply, knowing that there was no way in hell Joe could ever understand what it had been like. No one could who hadn't been there. "I was on point, first man into the village. Unbelievably hot. Sweat rolling down your back under your gear, raining into your eyes until your vision blurred and burned.

"Goats and chickens were scrabbling in the dirt and a couple of kids raced by with a battered soccer ball. Everything looked normal, but I just had a…feeling that something was wrong. A second later, I spotted a shooter in a doorway and turned to take him out." He paused for a sip of beer. "Jeff was right behind me. He spotted a sniper on the roof taking dead aim on my back. Jeff reacted fast. Took me down in a flying tackle. In a heartbeat, I was facedown on the street eating dirt while gunfire erupted all around us—and Jeff took the bullet meant for me."

Joe gave a heavy sigh, then slapped his hand against Rick's back. "I can't know how hard that was for you, buddy. Nobody can. But I'm grateful to Jeff."

Rick turned his head to smile at his old friend. "Yeah," he said. "So am I. Doesn't make it any easier to live with though."

"Can't imagine it would." A second later, Joe *whooped* and grabbed his pole. "Finally got a bite. Looks like fish for supper."

Rick watched Joe reel in a huge bass and thought that there was more he hadn't told his old friend. But what was said in the last few moments of Jeff Simpson's life was nobody else's business. In his mind, Rick heard his friend's strained whisper. Saw the pleading in his eyes and mentally added bricks to the wall he had built around his own heart that day.

Looking around him again, Rick felt the peace of his home ranch slide into him once more, easing the tattered edges of his soul. He took a breath of hot summer air and smiled to himself as he thought that, yeah, he was especially grateful to Jeff Simpson. And maybe that's the main reason Rick was going to leave the Corps. He didn't want to waste the life that Jeff had made possible.

He had a chance here, for more than he ever could have hoped for.

And he was going to take it.

Nine

Later that night, Sadie arrived back at the Price family home exhausted. She'd spent most of the day with Abby, decorating the club for the upcoming TCC Founder's Day dinner and dance. The annual event was the highlight of the year in Royal. Every member of the club would be there with their families, and Abby was bound and determined that this year would be something special.

And once Abby had her mind made up, Sadie thought with a smile, nothing could stop her. Not even Brad— who had, of course, shown up to protest everything they were doing.

"There's nothing wrong with the decorations we use every year," he had said, flatly challenging Abby to fight him on it.

He wasn't disappointed. Abby had climbed down from the ladder she was using to string twists of blue-and-gold crepe paper across the ceiling. Fisting her hands on her hips, she had faced him down.

"And then we can have the same food, the same wine and maybe even the same songs. Heck," Abby told him, "we don't even have to hold new dances, we can just videotape it and play it for the members every year. That way nothing will *ever* change and you'll finally be happy."

"Tradition means something in Texas," Brad had argued.

"Progress means something here, too," Abby countered. "Else we'd all still be riding horses and sending telegrams instead of emails!"

"Progress for progress's sake means nothing."

"Holding on to tradition because you're too *cowardly* to change means even less."

Sadie smiled just thinking about how her brother's face had frozen into a mask of frustration and barely reined-in temper. It was at that point that Brad had stormed from the club, looking as if he was about to explode. To be fair, Abby hadn't been doing any better by the time he left. It was a good hour and a half before Sadie's friend was able to talk without grumbling.

"The man just doesn't know who he's dealing with," Sadie said aloud.

She parked just opposite the front door, shut the engine off and dragged herself out of the car. She just stood there for a long minute, leaning against her SUV, looking up at the night sky, too tired to even walk the short distance to the house. Abby was a hard taskmaster, but Sadie knew this ball was going to be the best one ever.

But, time was passing and she still had to get inside and give the girls their bath and tuck them into bed.

Smiling, she forced herself toward the house only to stop when the front door was flung open. Her father stood in the open doorway, backlit by the hall light.

"Dad." Pleasure warred with a sinking sensation in her chest. She loved her father, but had figured out a long time ago that she was simply never going to be the daughter he wanted her to be. "When did you get home?"

"This afternoon." In his seventies, Robert Price was still a handsome man. His hair was mostly silver now, but he stood tall and straight and still carried the air of authority that had ruled Sadie's entire life.

Summoning a smile, she walked to him, went on her toes and kissed his cheek. "It's good to see you. Did you enjoy the Caribbean? Catch lots of fish?"

"I did," he said grudgingly. "Until I arrived home expecting to get a little time with my granddaughters only to find they're not here."

A ball of lead dropped into the pit of her stomach. Panic clutched at her heart. "Not here? What do you mean they're not here? They have to be here. Hannah babysat them for me today while I was at the club with Abby and—"

None of that mattered. Nothing mattered but finding her daughters. Where was Hannah? What could have happened?

She pushed past her father, headed for the staircase, to the girls' room, but her father's stern, no-nonsense voice stopped her dead.

"Don't bother, they're not in their room. Hannah tells me their *father* picked them up this afternoon and took them out to his ranch."

Slowly, Sadie turned around to face her father. His cool blue eyes were glinting with disapproval. The lead ball in her stomach iced over, then caught fire in a splintering shower of fury that swept through her in such a rush she could hardly draw a breath.

"He did *what?*"

"You heard me, Sadie. Rick Pruitt picked up the girls and took them home with him." Frowning, he asked, "Is this going to be a regular thing now? Are the girls going to be tossed back and forth between you two with no notice at all?"

"No," she told him, feeling the fire of her anger slide through her veins. "They're not."

"Hannah tells me that Pruitt has proposed to you."

"He did." Sadie was already walking out of the house, the heels of her sandals clacking noisily against the floor. Her father kept pace with her, out the door, down the porch steps and across the driveway.

Robert slapped one big hand on the car door to hold it closed when Sadie tried to wrestle it open. "And you turned him down?"

"I did."

"Why the hell would you do that?" he bellowed. "The Pruitt boy wouldn't have been my first choice, but you made that decision when you conceived your girls. Now he's here, ready to do his duty and you tell him *no*?"

"I am so bloody *sick* of the word *duty!*" Sadie shouted it and almost enjoyed seeing the shock written on her father's expression.

"I'll thank you not to raise your voice to me," Robert said coolly.

"It's the only way you'll ever hear me, Dad," she snapped. "I am no one's *duty.* I won't be forced into marriage. Not again."

This time, her father at least had the grace to look abashed. After all, it had been *he* who had forced her to marry Taylor. The man who had shown Sadie up close and personal just how humiliating a life could get.

"You owe it to your children—"

"That's right, Dad," she interrupted him and felt a rush of power inside her. She'd never stood up to him before and at that moment, she couldn't for the life of her fathom why not. "The girls are *my* children. Not yours. I'll make the decisions concerning them and I don't need any help. Not from you. Not from Rick Pruitt."

"You're obviously overwrought," Robert said.

"No, Dad," she countered, "I'm not overwrought. I'm *pissed*." She deliberately used a word she knew her father would find distasteful and felt another wash of freedom sweep through her.

"Sadie," her father said, his voice softer now, his eyes filled with concern.

No doubt, she told herself, he was convinced that she'd had a nervous breakdown. One padded room, coming up.

"I'm not crazy," she said. "I don't need to lie down. And I don't need you telling me what to do. Not anymore."

He opened and closed his mouth several times, but not a sound came out. For the first time in Sadie's memory, she was seeing her ever-so-perfect father speechless.

Sadie looked up at him and realized that the man who had run her life…the man whose approval she had sought for so long…no longer worried her. She was an adult now. A mother. And she didn't owe her father or any other damn person in Royal an explanation for anything she did.

"As for what happens with my girls, that's between me and Rick," she added. "Frankly, Dad, it's none of your business."

"Sadie!"

"Oh," she said, since she was on a roll and why stop now, "I'll be finding a place of my own. The girls and I can't stay here, Dad. I appreciate the interim help but it's time I stood on my own two feet again."

Deliberately, she peeled his fingers off the car door, opened it and slipped inside. She fired up the engine, rolled down her window and said, "I'm going to collect my daughters. I'll talk to you later."

And fatigue forgotten, she stepped on the gas until her tires squealed a protest as she peeled out of the driveway. A quick glance in her rearview mirror showed her that her father was still staring after her, clearly thunderstruck.

She smiled grimly.

He wouldn't be the *last* man she had it out with tonight.

Rick was ready for her.

He had been waiting for this confrontation since bringing the girls home to the ranch a few hours ago. Rick had to admit that without Sadie's housekeeper Hannah's cooperation, he never would have gotten away with it. Thankfully, though, the older woman was on his side in this mess. Also thankfully, Hannah had been with the Price family so long, was so much a mother to Sadie, that she wasn't worried about the possibility of losing her job for helping him.

It had been good, having his kids here for the afternoon. They had explored the stable, petted horses and fed carrots to the two ponies. They visited John Henry's golden retriever, who just happened to have given birth to a litter of pups the week before. The twins had been delighted with those puppies and were already busy claiming all eight of them.

Rick smiled, in spite of the battle that was looming in his immediate future. He was being sucked into a world filled with puppies, ponies and little girls' laughter.

And he loved it.

No way was he going to lose it.

When Sadie brought her car to a screeching halt out front, Rick opened the door and stood on the threshold, arms crossed over his chest, feet braced in a fighting stance. He knew she wouldn't listen to reason, so he had decided to try different ammunition in their private little war.

Looked like he had gotten her attention.

Sadie slammed the car door and shouted, "Where are they?"

"Right here," he said. "Where they belong."

She came around the front of the car like an avenging angel. He wouldn't have been surprised to see sparks flying off the top of her head, she was so furious.

Well, she should join the club because he was pretty mad himself. And he was fed up. Not a good combination.

"The girls *belong* with their mother."

"Wrong," Rick said as she closed on him, fury obviously firing every step she took. "They belong with their parents. Both of us."

She actually growled and threw her hands in the air helplessly. "We are not together! Damn it, Rick…"

"Hey, I tried to be reasonable. I tried to do the right thing. You don't want to hear it."

Her eyes widened and both blond eyebrows shot high on her forehead. "And you think *this* is the way to convince me to marry you? Kidnapping my daughters?"

He snorted derisively. "I didn't kidnap anybody. Those girls are just as much mine as yours."

She stomped up the front steps, stepping into the light thrown from the entryway. Illuminated against the backdrop of night, she looked even more beautiful than ever, he thought. Her long blond hair was loose around her shoulders. Her green T-shirt was wrinkled, her blue jeans were faded and soft and the heeled sandals she wore displayed toenails painted a deep crimson.

He wanted her so badly he could hardly breathe.

She pulled in a deep breath that did wonders for that T-shirt, then she lifted her chin and glared at him with all the freezing power of the ice princess he had once thought her to be.

"I want to see my daughters. Now."

"All you had to do was ask," he said.

"Why should I have to *ask* to see my own kids?" she snapped.

"Huh. Exactly what I've been asking myself," he told her.

Her mouth tightened up and he knew she was gritting her teeth in pure frustration. Good to see she was feeling a little of what he'd been dealing with lately.

"Are you going to let me pass?" she finally managed to grind out.

"Absolutely," he said and stepped to one side, allowing her to slip past him and into the house.

"Where are they?"

"In their room," he told her, following her as she headed for the wide staircase. "They're perfectly happy. Elena made them dinner, they've had a bath and now they're playing before bedtime."

"Their beds are at home."

"This is their home."

The wall along the stairwell was lined with dozens of framed photos. Of Rick's family, going back generations. This was the Pruitt home. Where Pruitt children were raised. Where his girls would grow up, he told himself firmly.

She stopped halfway up, pausing on a wide stair tread, and turned her head to fry him with another hot look. "You had no right."

Rick grabbed her arm and held her in place. "I had every right. I'm their father."

"You should have asked me."

"Right!" He laughed shortly without a trace of humor. "Like you enjoyed just asking me to arrange visits with the girls? I'll be damned if I'm going to ask permission every time I want to see my own kids."

She huffed out a breath, threw a quick glance at the top of the stairs, then turned her gaze back on him. "Rick, we're going to have to work this out. Legally. Visitation. Schedules."

"Do I look like the kind of man who's going to visit his kids according to a schedule some lawyer cooks up?" he asked her, keeping his voice low, so his daughters wouldn't hear him arguing with their mother.

Pulling her arm free of his grasp, she said shortly, "You won't have a choice. This is how things are done, Rick."

"Not in my family," he countered. "In my family, parents and children live together. They love each other. Those girls have a right to grow up on the ranch that will be theirs one day, Sadie. I want them to know it. To love it, like I do." He waved one hand at the wall behind her. "Look at those pictures, Sadie. That's family. The twins' family. They belong here."

"They will be here," she said, clearly trying to appease

him. "But they're not going to live here with you full-time, Rick. They'll be with me. They need their mother."

"Yeah, they do," he acknowledged. "But they need me, too."

He looked into those blue eyes and found himself fighting against his own instincts. Yes, he'd gone to her house to collect the children, not just because he'd wanted to be with them. But because he knew it would be a hard lesson for Sadie. He wasn't going to be cheated out of his kids' lives because their mother was too stubborn to do the right thing.

"I won't be bought off with weekends and part of the summer. I won't be a part-time visitor to my own children."

"I didn't say it would be like that."

"Yeah? How do you see it going, then?"

She sighed heavily and he only now noticed the signs of weariness about her. Her eyes weren't as clear as they usually were and there was a decided droop to her shoulders. Looked to him like she'd been getting by on very little sleep lately. Just like him. He didn't know whether to feel bad about that, or to be pleased knowing that she was as affected by this battle between them as he was.

He went with pleased.

Sagging against the wall, she looked at him for a long minute and finally shook her head. "I came over here ready to skin you alive for taking the girls without so much as telling me what you were up to."

"I can understand that."

"Now, I'm just relieved they're all right and truthfully, I'm too damn tired to fight with you *and* my father all in one night."

One of his eyebrows arched. "Your father? You took him on?"

"I did," she mused, a flicker of pride appearing briefly in her eyes. "In fact, I actually told him to mind his own business."

He whistled and felt a stirring of admiration for her. "Bet that came as a surprise."

"I'm sure," she admitted. "But he's not the only one I'm willing to stand up to, Rick."

"I get that, too." He moved in closer, bracing both hands on the wall on either side of her, effectively bracketing her in a cage of his arms. "But, Sadie, I'm not some trained dog you can tell to come and go as you please."

She laughed at the image. "Trust me, I never thought that of you. No one would."

"Good," he said, nodding. "And I'm not a civilized man, either, and you should know that about me. I'm a Texan and proud of it. I'm not the polite society type of man who'll step aside and say thanks very much for whatever scraps you're willing to hand me."

She sucked in a gulp of air and nodded. "I know."

"I won't be shut out of the girls' lives. I won't take second best. And I won't settle for less than everything I want."

Something hot flashed in the depths of her eyes and Rick felt a like fire start deep inside him. Even furious with her. Even so frustrated he could hardly think straight anymore, he still wanted her. Somehow, in the last couple of weeks, Sadie Price had become *essential* to him.

She was more than the girl he used to dream of on those tours of duty. She was more than that one hot night that had resulted in two children. She was more than his memories of a cool, untouchable girl in a prissy white dress.

Hell.

She was everything.

And suddenly, their battle wasn't as important as having her in his arms again.

"Stay with me tonight," he whispered, leaning in until his mouth was just a kiss from hers.

"I don't think—"

"Good," he interrupted her quickly. "Don't think. Just react, Sadie. To what's between us."

"What would that solve?"

"Why does it have to solve anything?" He kissed her, lightly, delicately, his teeth pulling gently at her bottom lip until she was nearly whimpering. When he let up, he raised his head, looked her in the eye and said, "The girls are ready for bed. You don't want to go back and fight with your father again. So stay. *Stay,* Sadie.…"

Closing her eyes briefly, she reached out and wrapped her fists in his black T-shirt, crumpling the fabric. "This isn't why I came here."

"So? Let it be why you don't leave."

"Daddy!"

He jerked his head up at the sound of Wendy's plaintive wail demanding his presence. Then he realized he could already tell the difference in the twins' voices and he smiled. They were a part of him, those girls. His flesh and blood. His family.

"Daaaaadddddddy…" Now Gail sang out, stretching that one word into about a dozen syllables and Rick's grin spread until Sadie couldn't help but return it. Would he ever get tired of hearing his children calling for him? He didn't think so.

"What do you say?" he asked, pushing off from the

wall to fold his fingers around her much smaller hand. "How about both of their parents read them bedtime stories? *Together.*"

She looked down at their joined hands, then back up, into his eyes. He wished he knew what she was thinking because there was pleasure mixed with sorrow in her eyes and that kind of combination could give a man gray hair before his time.

But a moment later, she nodded. "Together. Tonight, at least."

"That's a start," he said and led her up the stairs to where their twin daughters were waiting.

Ten

An hour later, the girls were fast asleep and Sadie was stretched out on Rick's bed. She had to get up and take a shower, but for the moment, she was too tired to even attempt it.

She ran her hand over the heavy, dark red quilt beneath her and felt her insides tremble at what she knew would be coming soon. Maybe this was another huge mistake, she admitted silently. But at the moment, there was nowhere else she'd rather be.

Amazing that this man could infuriate her to the point of mayhem and in the next instant, kiss her until all she could think about was ripping off her clothes and falling into his arms.

"This is *not* a rational way to live," she murmured aloud.

Sitting up, she scooted to the edge of the bed and gave a quick look around. Rick was off in the kitchen getting them something to eat, so she had at least a few minutes to herself.

This wasn't the room she had been in only the week before. He had moved his things into the master suite and she knew that was a sure sign that he meant what he'd said about leaving the Marines and coming home to stay.

There was a bay window at the front of the room and a window seat at its base. A stone fireplace was on one side of the room and on either side of the massive hearth stood floor-to-ceiling bookshelves. There were two comfy chairs drawn up in front of the now cold fireplace and the bed was big enough for four people.

It was a sumptuous room, somehow homey and sensual all at once.

Her thoughts dissolved as she heard the distinctive sound of rushing water. Sliding off the bed, she walked across the room and entered a bathroom that most women would have killed for.

Acres of sky-blue tile with white accents gleamed in the soft light of dozens of lit candles. An oversize tub was frothing with bubbles and a mirror that stretched the length of the room reflected those dancing flames—and the man who had lit all of the candles.

She looked at Rick. "Where did you come from?"

He jerked his thumb at the closed door behind him and grinned. "It's a sitting room my mom used when she wanted to get away from my dad for a while without really leaving the house."

"Handy," she said and looked longingly at the steam and bubbles drifting up out of the tub.

"Come on." He held out one hand to her. "A bath'll make you feel better."

"It'll probably put me to sleep," she warned him.

"Oh, I don't think so," he said. "See, that tub's more than big enough for *two*."

Heat slapped at her and jolted the last bits of fatigue from her system in an instant. Her body flushed and that now familiar, damp ache settled between her thighs.

He smiled at her and what she read in his eyes made that ache pound in time with her heartbeat. Yet, she couldn't resist teasing. "You mean big, bad Texan men take bubble baths?"

"Darlin', if we've got company like you, there's a lot we'll put up with."

He walked toward her and every step he took made the anticipation inside Sadie ratchet up another notch. By the time he reached her, she was hardly able to swallow past the knot of need in her throat.

"Now," he said, taking hold of the hem of her T-shirt to drag it up and over her head, "let's get you undressed and into that tub."

As good as his word, in seconds, Sadie was naked and he turned her so that she was facing herself in the mirror. Any embarrassment she might have felt drained away in an instant. She looked into her own eyes and saw the flash of heat there. Then she lifted her gaze to the reflection of the man who stood behind her.

He covered her breasts with his hands, and as she watched their mirrored images, Sadie felt tingles of excitement light up inside her. His hands were big and tanned and the palms were calloused. She caught her breath and held it.

"Now," he whispered, dipping his head to the curve of her neck, "I want you to watch me touch you."

He looked into the mirror and met her reflected gaze. When she nodded, he slid one hand down her body, along the curve of her waist, back over her abdomen to the juncture of her thighs. A pale brush of blond hair was all that stood between him and the object of his quest.

Sadie couldn't draw another breath. Her head was fuzzy, her legs were weak and all she could do was squirm against him. She felt the cold chill of his belt buckle against her spine and the coarse rub of his jeans. But more importantly, she felt the hard ridge of his body pressed into her bottom.

He sighed as she moved against him, but shook his head at her in the mirror. "First you, darlin'. First I want to watch you come for me. I want *you* to see us together. To know what I see when I look at you. To see my hands on your body. To feel my mouth on your skin."

Every word he whispered was another match adding to the inferno burning within her. Reaching back, Sadie hooked one arm around his neck, holding his head close, even as she parted her thighs for him and silently begged him to ease the throbbing ache at her core.

His gaze caught hers in the mirror as he slowly, slowly lowered his hand to the heart of her body. The first brush of his fingers against her sex brought a whimpered sigh scraping from Sadie's throat. She laid her head back against his shoulder, kept her gaze locked on their mirrored images and concentrated on what he was making her feel.

His fingers moved over her flesh, sliding back and forth, dipping into her heat only to slide out again. His thumb smoothed across that one perfect nub of sensation until Sadie was gasping and writhing against him. Still she watched, unable to look away, unable to tear her eyes from the image of his hands on her body.

With his free hand, he tugged and tweaked at one of her nipples, creating a tangled mass of desires that threatened to choke her with their strength. She was a shivering, trembling knot of raw nerves as he continued to stroke her innermost flesh in the most intimate caresses.

Again and again, he delved deep within her. First one finger and then two, taking her higher, pushing her faster until she was twisting against him and fighting for air as desperately as she fought to reach the climax building within.

"There it is," Rick whispered, obviously sensing her release was close. "Grab it, Sadie. Take what I can give you and let me watch your pleasure."

"Rick...Rick..." She shuddered, gasped, pulled in a desperate, frantic gulp of air and rocked her hips against his hand in a frenzied rush toward completion. "Touch me harder," she whispered. "More...more..."

He looked into her reflected eyes and gave her what she needed. He stroked that nub of flesh where so much pleasure was caged until she splintered in his arms and called his name helplessly.

Minutes, hours might have passed for all Sadie knew. Her hips were still moving on his hand and she didn't want him to ever stop touching her. She was spent. Sated. And still wanted him.

He turned her in his arms, wrapping her up close to him and kissing her until he couldn't breathe, think. Rick thought he had known want before, but those few moments with her, watching her pleasure move across her face, hearing her breathless cries had inflamed him past the point of reason.

Tongues tangling together, hands moving, exploring, bodies pressed together, they stood, locked into an inseparable unit in the middle of the plush bathroom. The world fell away until it was only the two of them with the constant rush and stream of hot water filling an enormous tub to keep them company. The air was hot and sultry. The steam from the tub misted around them like shadow dancers.

Rick tore his mouth from hers, then quickly rid himself of his own clothing. Sweeping her up into his arms, he carried her into the tub and sat down in the hot, frothy water, cradling her on his lap. Her breasts pushed into his chest. Her wet, silky body moved against his. Her hands slid up his neck and framed his face as she kissed him with a heat that was more enveloping than anything that had gone on before.

As if they had each resigned themselves to the inevitable. As if the harsh words between them were forgotten and the problems still waiting for them were resolved.

They were lost, both of them, and together they were found.

He reached down, took her legs and parted them over him. She straddled him easily and moved quickly to take him inside her. There was no slow, deliberate torture this time. No. Now, the torture was being apart. Their only salvation was to join. To lock their two separate bodies into one. To claim the magic that they could only find together.

She impaled herself on him, letting her head fall back as he filled her. Rick kept his hands at her slender waist, then slid them to her hips. He moved her on him, helping her set a fast, breathless rhythm designed to push them both over the edge as quickly as possible.

They'd had the prelude.

Now they each wanted completion.

Still the raging torrent of water rushed into the tub. The jets on the sides of the massive tub pulsed, driving that water into his back, across her skin. More sensations added to those that were born with a touch.

She rode him desperately, rising and falling, releasing him and claiming him again and again. And through it all, her gaze remained fixed with his. As if nothing else existed beyond this room. Beyond this small sea of water that held them in a hot, foaming embrace.

Rick's breath was hard and fast. His needs erupting inside him, quickening with every move she made. He leaned forward, taking first one of her nipples then the other into his mouth, working them with his teeth and tongue. Nibbling. Suckling. Taking her needs into him and giving them back to her mixed with his own.

Her breath sang around him like a damn symphony. She sighed and his heart fisted. She moaned and he got even harder. She twisted her body on his and he felt the tug of release pulling at him.

"Go, darlin'," he urged, rearing back to look up at her fierce, beautiful face. "Take me as only you can."

"I want to watch you now," she said, each word coming in a short, hard gasp. "Come first. I'll follow."

Her gaze locked on him and Rick did as she asked. He released the taut reins of control, surrendered to her heat and allowed his body to erupt into hers.

He called her name on a harsh, guttural groan and before his body had emptied itself, he felt the first tremors shake through her and knew she had kept her word and followed after him.

Sadie slumped against him, her breathing ragged. Rick wrapped his arms around her, murmured her name and even as he held her close, he silently vowed never to let her go.

An hour later, they were lying together in his bed and Sadie was more confused than ever. She ran her fingertips up and down his arm, draped across her middle. She'd come to the ranch tonight, half ready to have him arrested for kidnapping or, at the very least, to hit him with something heavy.

Instead, she'd landed in his bed, in his arms and she couldn't bring herself to regret it. So what did that mean? Her feelings were so convoluted, her mind so tired of going over the same arguments and finding no answers.

"You're thinking," he whispered, tugging her closer.

Her back to his front, she felt his heat sliding into her body. His breath brushed against her hair and the steady thud of his heartbeat pounded in time with hers.

"C'mon, Sadie," he prompted, "I can practically hear the wheels in your mind turning. Tell me what you're thinking."

She turned her head so she could look back at him. Her heart turned over in her chest as her eyes locked with his. How had he become so important to her in so short a time?

Or was it that short? she wondered. Had they been heading here all their lives? Was the crush she'd had on him as a girl only the seeds of what was flowering between them now?

Oh, God. Her stomach pitched as she realized the hard truth she'd been managing to ignore for days. Maybe years.

She was in love with Rick Pruitt.

Her heartbeat sped up and her mouth went dry.

There was no other explanation for her behavior. Why else would she have turned down his marriage proposals time after time? If she didn't love him, she might have married him if only for the sake of the girls.

But loving him, how could she do that? How could she sentence herself to a half life where *she* loved and wasn't loved in return? He'd made no secret of the fact that he wasn't interested in love. What he wanted was his children and a great sex life with her. It wasn't enough.

Her eyes closed as her heart wrenched in her chest. Misery rose up and choked her.

When did this happen? That first night when they made the twins? Or was it before, when a teenaged Rick had smiled at her? Or was it, she asked herself, when he'd stormed back into her life demanding to be a part of it? Or maybe, she thought, it had happened when she had first seen him with their girls? Watched the wonder in his eyes, the pure love radiating from him for those two tiny charmers?

Oh, it didn't matter when it had happened. All that mattered now was the fact that she was in love with a man who felt nothing for her but desire.

Misery spilled into despair. Loving alone was a sentence of loneliness and she didn't see a way out of it.

"Okay," he said, dipping his head to kiss her temple. "Now I have to know what's making you frown when you should be feeling as good as I do right now."

"I do feel good," she said quietly, knowing that statement for being only a half truth. "But—"

He dropped his head onto the pillow. "Knew there had to be a 'but' in there somewhere."

"How can there not be?" She turned around, braced her forearms on his bare chest. Looking into his eyes, she saw everything she could ever want and knew that unless he loved her, too, she would never have any of it. "Nothing's been solved, Rick. We still have a major problem."

"*You* have the problem, darlin'," he said, tapping her nose with his finger. "Me, I'm a happy man. I know what I want. I know what I've *got*." He ran one hand over her back in a slow stroke that had her arching into his touch like a cat.

Sighing, Sadie told herself to get a grip and try to talk. Her body, though, kept turning on her. "I was furious with you today."

"Yeah." He wiggled his eyebrows at her. "May all our fights end just like this one did."

He gave her a quick squeeze and Sadie felt a well of sorrow fill her. Realizing that she was in love should have made her happy. But all she could see was more pain headed her way. And still, she had to know for sure.

"Rick, why do you want to marry me?"

"What?"

"Simple question," she said, hanging onto a slender thread of hope. Maybe he did love her. Maybe he had just assumed that she would know that when he proposed. Maybe there was still a chance that she could have the man—the life—she wanted.

Because she couldn't be a wife only because she was a mother. She couldn't marry a man who simply *desired* her, either. There had to be more, she thought.

There had to be love.

Rick studied her face for a long moment, then used the tips of his fingers to smooth her hair back behind her ear. Emotions churned in his eyes, but they appeared and disappeared so quickly, she couldn't identify them. All she could do was wait and pray that he would say the one thing she needed to hear.

"You know why," he said, and that bubble of hope inside her popped. "We're good together, Sadie. We make a good match. We've got kids and we should be a family."

"We should," she agreed sadly, knowing that it would never happen. Not this way. Not the way he wanted it to.

With no other options open to her, Sadie couldn't stay. She pushed out of his arms, slid off the bed and walked to the chair where she'd dropped her clothes.

He sat up, quilt pooled at his waist. In the soft lamplight, his skin looked like burnished bronze and his brown eyes were shadowed and dark. "What're you doing? What's wrong?"

"I'm going home," she said softly.

"Damn it, Sadie." He jumped out of bed and walked to her, grabbing her arms when he reached her. "Don't do this to us anymore. This game between us is getting old."

"I agree," she said, "and I don't want to play anymore. But, Rick, it isn't *me* doing this."

She tugged her T-shirt over her head and stuffed her arms through the sleeves.

"Well, it's not me. I'm not the one running away."

She cocked her head and looked up at him. "Aren't you?"

"What's that supposed to mean?"

Sadie sighed and lifted both hands in surrender. "Never mind. It's nothing."

"Then why are you leaving?"

"Because you can't give me what I need."

"Bull." He glared down at her and his dark eyes fixed on her mercilessly. "Tell me what you're talking about and I'll get it for you."

"Love."

It was as if the world took a breath and held it. The silence between them was so profound, Sadie heard the drip of the water faucet in the bathroom. The soft sighs their children made, drifting through the baby monitor. The silent crack of her own heart breaking.

"Well," she said, when she couldn't bear the quiet any longer. "That put an end to the conversation, didn't it?"

"Sadie…"

She read regret in his eyes and that tore at her. She didn't want his pity. She wanted his love and, clearly, she wasn't going to get it. Shaking her head, she stepped into her underwear then snatched up her jeans. "I have to go."

"Sadie, I *care* for you," he said tightly. He reached for her, then let his hand drop before he actually touched her. "More than I have for anyone in my life. Isn't that enough?"

She wished it could be. More than anything, she'd love to hold him and have him lead her back to bed. To wake up every morning with his arms wrapped around her. To build the family she had always dreamed of. Yes, she wished caring could be enough. But it wasn't.

"No," she said, flinging her hair back out of her face to look at him. "It's not. I deserve more, Rick. *We* deserve more. We deserve love."

He pushed one hand across the top of his head and bit back a curse. "How do you even know what love *is?*"

She smiled sadly. "You know it when you feel it."

"Well, that's clear as mud."

Now it was her turn to reach for him. She cupped his cheek in her palm. "I love you, Rick. Maybe I always have."

He caught her hand and held it to his face. "Then—"

"No, one person in love isn't a marriage," she said, "it's a recipe for disaster. Remember, I was married to a man who didn't love me. I can't do that again."

"I'm not him."

"No, you're really not," she agreed. "You're a better

man than he ever was. But the next time I get married, it will be because I've found someone who loves me."

"You don't know what you're asking."

"Yeah," she insisted, "I do."

He released her hand and shook his head. "No. You throw the word *love* around, but you don't know. You don't know the pain it brings…what havoc it can cause. Well, I do. I saw what love can do to a man while I was deployed."

Sadie was watching him and saw his features tighten and his eyes fill with shadows. The old pain and secrets she had once glimpsed in those depths were shining there, glittering like diamonds. Every instinct she had urged her to comfort him, but she didn't. Instead, she waited to hear him out. To find out what exactly was at the bottom of his refusal to give and receive love.

He rubbed his jaw as if trying to hold his words in. He shifted his gaze to the wide window and the night beyond as if he couldn't bear to look at her anymore. Several long moments passed and Sadie actually *saw* him regain control.

His shoulders squared, his chin lifted and his eyes narrowed. She wondered if he was ever going to explain, or if he was simply going to let what was between them end without ceremony or reason.

Finally, though, she had her answer when he turned his head toward her. "Love tears people up, Sadie. It makes them miserable. It ruins lives," he said.

It didn't make any sense, but she could see that he believed what he was saying, so her heart ached. "How can you think that?"

"One of my best friends, Jeff, he died during my last tour." He turned his face back to the window and his reflection stared back at him. "He died saving my life and you know what he said with his last breath? 'Tell Lisa I'm sorry. Tell her I love her.'"

Tears filled her eyes and spilled unheeded down her cheeks. Pity swamped her—for Rick, Jeff and mostly, the much-loved Lisa. Yet even knowing what Lisa had lost, Sadie envied her. Though she had lost the man she loved, she had also been truly loved by him. And that was a gift too few people would ever realize.

She looked into the gleaming black surface of the night-shrouded windowpane and met his stony stare. "I'm sorry, Rick. I really am. But I don't understand. What's so horrible about your friend's last words? His love for his wife was beautiful."

"Beautiful." A short, harsh laugh scraped from his throat. "He died in torment because he knew he was leaving Lisa alone. He knew loving her wouldn't be enough and his death was going to kill her."

"Rick…"

He turned, grabbed his own jeans and drew them on with jerky movements. Then he flashed her a hard look. "If he hadn't loved someone, he could have died in peace. He wouldn't have been panic-stricken trying to tell me what he needed Lisa to know. He—" His voice broke off and he shook his head again, then folded his arms across his chest in a classic pose of defensiveness.

Her heart was breaking—for Rick, and for the Jeff she would never meet. But she had to try to get past this. To find a way to make him see that love wasn't a curse, it was a rare gift.

"And you think he regretted loving his wife?"

"I'm betting he regretted it on that day. In that dusty street, in those last few minutes. Yeah." He stalked across the room to the cold fireplace. Fisting his hands on the old oak mantle, he stared into the empty hearth.

"Yeah. I think he did regret it. But it was too late. For him. *And* for Lisa."

"So to save yourself ever feeling that helpless kind of pain, you'll just never love anyone?"

He didn't lift his gaze, but he nodded. "That's right."

"What about the girls?" She walked to his side and waited for him to look at her before adding, "You love them."

His mouth curved in a bitter smile. "That's different and you know it."

"I know you love them, so you're risking the same kind of misery you said your friend experienced. Wanting to be there for them and not being able to. Wanting to tell them everything you're feeling and failing at that, too." She laid one hand on his shoulder and felt him flinch at her touch. "So I ask you, would it be better to never love them at all?"

He turned his gaze from hers and focused again on the empty hearth and the battered old iron grate. "You don't understand."

"No," she said softly, "I don't. I'll never understand turning your back on love because you're afraid of what might happen."

His head snapped up at her choice of the word *afraid* and she knew she'd struck a nerve. "It isn't fear, Sadie. It's a rational decision—and mine to make."

There was a coolness in his eyes now. A distance she'd never seen there before and it saddened her more than she could say. But at the same time, there was a very slender ribbon of hope remaining. It wasn't that he *didn't* love her. He was *refusing* to love her. And that she could fight against. All she had to do was make him change that stubborn mind of his.

Now that she knew what was at the root of his refusal

to love, she knew she'd be able to get through to him eventually. But for right now, there was nothing more she could do.

Suddenly she was more tired than she'd ever been. "I'm going home now, Rick. I'll be back in the morning to pick up the girls."

"Fine," he murmured.

A little stung that he was more than willing to let her leave, Sadie walked out of the room, but couldn't help pausing on the threshold to look back at him. Still hunched over the fireplace, he looked more alone than she'd ever seen him.

Sadie's heart broke a little further. She hated to leave him like this, but maybe it was a good thing. Maybe he'd take out his memories and examine them more closely. If he did, Sadie thought he would discover that, yes, his friend Jeff had lost a lot on that last day—but in loving his wife, he had shown Rick what was really important.

Rick had once told her that he never gave up. Well, she wouldn't give up on him, either. If there was a way to crash past the defenses he had built up around his heart, she told herself as she left the room to walk down the dimly lit hall, she would find it.

Rick heard her leave, and his every instinct urged him to go after her. To never let her walk away. He *needed* her, damn it. He was empty without her.

And in the silent turmoil of his own mind, he heard Jeff's voice again. *Tell Lisa I love her.*

Eleven

Two days later, the Founder's Day dinner and dance at the Texas Cattleman's Club was a success.

That fact would no doubt drive Brad crazy, Sadie thought, but she couldn't help feeling proud. She and Abby and the other women had really worked hard to shake things up a little this year.

There were new decorations—blue-and-gold crepe paper and matching balloons hanging from the ceiling. There were pictures of past parties—blown up poster size—decorating the walls and instead of a boring, sit-down meal, there were two buffet tables practically groaning with delectable choices.

Waiters from the club stood behind the tables making sure the trays were kept full and the steamers were hot. People were laughing, talking, moving around the room and visiting—instead of being trapped at their linen-covered tables as in previous years.

Everyone seemed to be having a wonderful time. Everyone who wasn't her. Idly, she smoothed one hand down the front of her crimson, floor-length gown. She'd looked all over until she had found the perfect dress for tonight—because she had wanted to knock Rick off his feet.

The minute she saw this dress, she'd known it was the one. It molded to her body like a second skin. The neckline was cut deeply enough to display just the right amount of her cleavage and in the back, the fabric swept down to display her entire spine, right down to the top of her behind.

She felt sexy. Beautiful.

And lonely, she thought. *Don't forget lonely.*

Abby was across the room, easy to spot with her long, dark red hair done on top of her head to complement the emerald-green Grecian style gown she wore. Not far from Abby, Brad was holding court with a few of his best friends and judging from her brother's expression, he was probably campaigning again for club president.

She spotted her father in a corner talking to one of the older club members, and Sadie knew that Robert Price was no doubt trying to drum up votes for his son.

After all, *Brad* wasn't the disappointment, *she* was.

Walking to the bar, Sadie caught snatches of conversation as she went.

"I hear that Bradford Price is going to vote to keep the club just the way it is."

"A little change never hurt anybody."

"I don't care for change myself, but I do admit that Abby Langley did a fine job with the party."

"Oh, my, look at Sadie Price…"

Her steps faltered a little, just long enough for her to hear the end of that sentence.

"…She's been keeping company with Rick Pruitt. You know…the *father* of those two little girls? Poor mites."

"If he's their father, why doesn't he marry their mother for pity's sake?"

Good question, Sadie thought and lifted her chin a bit higher as she wended her way through the meandering crowd. The curse of a small town, she told herself, was that absolutely everyone knew your business. The blessing of a small town? Everybody knew your business. The same people who gossiped and spread rumors were also the first ones to show up when there was a call for help.

She knew what she would be letting herself in for in moving back home. And she was prepared for it. All she needed was a little vodka to help her over tonight's bumps in the road.

People carrying loaded plates headed for the tables and waiters drifted through the crowd with bottles of champagne to refill empty glasses. But Sadie wasn't in the mood for a celebratory drink. All she wanted was a little liquor, then she'd get something to eat, say hello to a few people and call it an early night.

If Rick wasn't here, there was no point in her staying.

While she waited at the bar, she watched as a dozen or so couples on the dance floor swayed and spun to the music pouring through the speakers. It was an old song. One of her father's favorites. Frank Sinatra singing about a summer wind.

Unconsciously, she began to sway in time with the music only to jolt to a stop when a voice from behind her spoke up.

"Can I have this dance?"

Her heart did a fast gallop and her mouth went dry as

dust. Sadie turned around slowly and looked up into the warm brown eyes she had most hoped to see that night.

"Rick." He wore his dress blues uniform for the formal occasion and Sadie thought he had never looked more handsome. More...imposing.

Torn between excitement and dread, Sadie didn't know what to think of the way he was looking at her— as if he could devour her with the power of his stare alone.

She hadn't seen him in two days. Not since she'd left him alone in his room in the middle of the night. Her stomach had been in perpetual knots since then and her mind was constantly churning, dragging up one impossible scenario after another.

He loved her, he didn't love her; they married, she died a lonely spinster and he a bitter old man.

Even her normally even-tempered daughters seemed to sense that their mommy was tangled up in her own cascading emotions. As if in sympathy, Wendy and Gail had both been whiny and irritable.

And asking for their daddy.

She knew how they felt because Sadie wanted him too. Now, here he was. And a more gorgeous man she had never seen. The infuriating hardhead.

"Dance with me, Sadie," he said softly, taking her hand in both of his.

She nodded and allowed him to tug her onto the dance floor. Sadie knew that most of the people in the place were watching them, hoping for more fuel for the gossip train. But she didn't care. All she cared about now was the feel of his arm sliding around her. The touch of his warm hand on the small of her back. The feel of her fingers caught in his firm but gentle grip.

He moved into the dance, steering them onto the

middle of the floor and as the music swelled around them, Sadie felt the pain of the last couple of days fall away.

"I've missed you," he said, voice just loud enough for her to hear.

"I've missed you, too." She looked up into his eyes and realized that the cool indifference that had so cut at her the other night was gone.

What did that mean?

"You stayed away on purpose, didn't you?" he asked, spinning her into a tight turn.

"No, I—"

He smiled. "It's okay, Sadie. Probably a good thing you did. Gave me time to think. And there was a lot to think about."

Her heart was stuttering in her chest and the pit of her stomach swarmed with what felt like giant bats. "Come to any conclusions?"

"A few." The song ended and another slow, dreamy romantic tune began.

Rick didn't miss a beat. He kept dancing, holding her even closer as the couples around them danced and laughed.

"Care to tell me what they were?" she asked, silently congratulating herself on being so poised—when what she wanted to do was grab him and kiss him and demand that he love her as much as she loved him.

"I'm getting to it," he said with a half smile that sent shivers of appreciation over her skin.

Glancing across the clubhouse briefly, he turned his gaze back to her. "You remember I once told you that life was all about change?"

"Yes…"

"Well, something occurred to me after you left the other night."

"What?"

"That some change just isn't worth it."

Her heart fell, but then he started talking again.

"Like you leaving me for instance," he said, gaze fixed firmly on hers. "Like me losing the chance to be with you. That's the kind of change that could kill a man."

A ping of guilt came and went in the space of a heartbeat. "I couldn't stay, Rick—"

"I know." He interrupted her, brought her close for a brief, hard hug, then bent his head to hers. "I mean, I understand. Sadie, I want you to know you mean more to me than anything else in this world."

Again, her heartbeat quickened. Honestly, she thought wildly, the ups and downs of this conversation were making her a nervous wreck.

"I'm glad, Rick. But—"

"Not finished," he said, another half smile curving his mouth into a temptation.

"Okay…"

Quiet conversations rippled across the crowded room. The music went on, sliding into one romantic tune after another. The subtle clatter of plates and glasses was nothing more than a vague distraction.

"See," he continued, staring down into her eyes, "I had a meeting with someone yesterday."

"Who?"

He shook his head. "Doesn't matter. What does, is that I realized something important."

Oh, God… If she got her hopes up now only to see them shattered, Sadie thought it might just destroy her. So she tried not to read anything into the gleam in his eyes. But she couldn't keep from wishing for what she most wanted.

"You were right," he told her and this time when the music ended, he steered her off the dance floor and into a shadowed corner of the room.

"Three words every woman loves to hear," she said, bracing her back against the cool, plastered wall.

"I've got three more for you."

She inhaled sharply and felt a warning sting of tears in her eyes. Looking up into his eyes, she saw warmth, she saw passion, and she saw...

"I love you."

Sadie clapped one hand over her mouth to keep from—what? Shrieking? Gasping?

He pulled her hand free, kissed the palm, then drew her into his arms, pressing her entire length to him. "Ah, God, Sadie. I was an idiot."

She nodded, smiling through the tears that brimmed in her eyes and trembled on her lashes.

"I'm over it," he said, smiling as he reached into his jacket pocket. Pulling out that velvet jeweler's box, he opened the lid and showed her the diamond. "So, Sadie Price, will you marry me now?"

"Try to stop me," she said and held out her hand for him to slide that platinum and diamond ring onto her fourth finger.

The oversize stone flashed with light buried in its depths, but when Rick leaned in to kiss her, she saw real stars and felt her life click perfectly into place.

That lasted about an hour.

Which was when the big argument started.

Sadie was showing Abby her ring when Brad stormed up to them.

"Are you serious?" he demanded, ignoring his sister to focus on the redhead glaring at him. "I heard you were actually thinking about running for president of the club. It's a joke, right?"

Whoever was in charge of the stereo shut it off and the abrupt absence of music was startling enough to have everyone in the room turning to watch what would happen next.

With Rick at her side, Sadie spoke softly. "Brad, maybe now isn't the time…"

"You stay out of this," her brother snapped.

"Hey now!" Rick warned, stepping in between Sadie and her brother. "You want to watch how you talk to my fiancée."

"Fiancée?"

More excited whispers raced through the crowd and Sadie rolled her eyes. Trust her brother to speak up and spoil her having the chance to make her own announcement.

"You're getting married?"

"Since when?" her father demanded as he came up to join the fracas.

"Since about an hour ago," Sadie told him proudly and waved her ring in her father's face.

"It's about time," Robert said, fixing Rick with a disapproving stare.

"This isn't about Sadie," Brad said, his voice rising to carry over the crowd's murmuring. "This is about Abby Langley and just what she thinks she's up to."

"I don't owe you an explanation for anything, Bradford Price," Abby told him.

"I want a damn answer," Brad ground out as a few of the older club members drifted up to stand behind his father.

Abby went toe-to-toe with him, tipped her head back and speared him with a glare. "I was going to wait until next week to say this, but you want an answer now? Fine. It's not a joke. I *am* running." Then she raised her voice to match his so that everyone present would hear her. "I'm officially declaring myself a candidate for president of the TCC. Anyone besides Brad have a problem with that?"

Instantly, the crowd was electrified and divided into two separate camps. Snatches of comments rose up into the air.

"Good for her!"

"A *woman* running the club?"

"That Abby was always a troublemaker."

At that comment, Abby and Sadie both turned to fire off angry glances at the speaker. The older man who had spoken a bit too loudly slunk back into the crowd.

"He's just saying what everyone's thinking," Brad told her.

"Is that right? Well, maybe it's time for a troublemaker. At least then," Abby countered, "every meeting won't be so boring the members fall asleep half way through."

"*This* is what's wrong with women being admitted to the club as members," Brad declared and several of the men nodded. "Change for change's sake is stupid. You want to ditch tradition in favor of progress and I don't know if you've noticed or not, but nobody agrees with you."

"I do," Sadie announced.

He brushed her comment away with the wave of a hand. "No one asked you what you thought, Sadie."

"Maybe you should have, Bradford Price. Instead, you're behaving like a spoiled child," Sadie snapped, pushing past Rick to face her brother. "If this is how you behave, then you shouldn't be the president!"

"Sadie!" Robert Price's horrified gasp carried over the crowd.

Sadie knew she'd stepped in it now, siding with an outsider against a member of her own family—in public no less. But Brad was wrong. Why shouldn't she call him on it?

"Sadie's right," Rick said. "You're being a jackass, man. This isn't the way to handle things. You don't want her to be president? Then win the election."

She looked up at her marine and grinned. It felt wonderful to have his support. To know that he would always be by her side. When he looked down at her, she whispered, "My hero."

"My pleasure," he assured her.

"Oh, for God's sake." Brad looked disgusted with all of them. His gaze snapped from Rick to Sadie and, finally, to Abby. "I plan to win. Lady, get used to the idea of losing."

"We'll see, won't we?" Abby said with a sneer.

"You want war, Abby? You got it," Brad said.

Bradford Price was still furious days after the Founder's Day dance. Abby Langley had become the proverbial thorn in his side and he hadn't yet found the way to dig her out. Still, to be fair, it wasn't just Abby getting under his skin. He was on edge all the damn time now. Getting anonymous, vaguely threatening letters in the mail was enough to make any man uneasy.

Which was why he was here at the TCC today. He'd decided to be proactive in figuring out who it was that was harassing him. From the corner of his eye, he caught movement and glance up in time to see Rick Pruitt leaving the club dining room. Briefly, Brad wondered if the man was the right one for his sister. But a second later, he reminded himself that *that* particular problem wasn't what concerned him today.

He looked at the two men at the table with him. Mitch Taylor he'd known most of his life. The interim president of the TCC, Mitch was a star in Texas football, home now recuperating from an injury. Mitch's cool brown eyes met Brad's and he nodded. Mitch already knew about the letters and had suggested he use the club lounge for this meeting with the man Brad hoped would solve the issue.

Zeke Travers was new in town, but he was Darius Franklin's new partner in his security firm. So that was a hell of a recommendation as far as Brad was concerned. If Darius trusted the man, Brad knew he could, too.

Zeke's head was shaved, and his brown eyes were sharp as he watched Brad, waiting. His white shirt accented his dark skin and his black slacks had a crease sharp enough to draw blood. He was all business and Brad could appreciate that.

"Look," he said, lowering his voice as he braced his forearms on the table. "Mitch knows why I asked you to meet me here, Zeke. I've got a situation."

"Tell me."

"I've been getting letters." He dipped one hand into his jacket pocket and drew out a single sheet of paper. Sliding it across the table, he waited as Zeke picked it up and read it.

It didn't take long. The letters were short. Always the same.

Your secret will be revealed.

Zeke's eyes narrowed as he folded the letter again. "Can I hang on to this?"

"Sure."

"How many have you been getting?"

"One a day for weeks now," Brad admitted, shoving one hand through his hair. "I'll admit it's starting to get to me."

Zeke nodded. "I'd be surprised if it wasn't. You want me to look into this for you?"

"That's why we're here," Mitch said, speaking up for the first time. "Darius is a friend of ours and he trusts you."

Zeke smiled briefly and gave a quick nod to Mitch. "He does. So can you."

Brad nodded.

"I'll see what I can do with this," Zeke told him. "I'll get the guys in the lab to go over it. See what they can find out."

Brad released a breath he hadn't realized he'd been holding. It was good to have someone on his side in this. "Appreciate it," he said.

Zeke held out his hand and Brad shook it. "Don't get your hopes up, though. This letter's been handled so much, it's doubtful we'll get much information on it."

When Brad solemnly nodded, Zeke added, "But it's a start."

Standing up, he said simply, "I'll be in touch."

He left and Brad thought that with Zeke Travers in his corner, he could breathe a little easier.

Royal was taking sides.

Taking the twins shopping on Main Street, Sadie was stopped a half a dozen times by women who were absolutely furious with their husbands. All of the women wanted to talk about Abby running for president of the TCC and were thinking of ways they could help get her elected.

The men were up in arms, too. Her own father was hardly speaking to her and she hadn't seen Brad since the night of the dance, three days ago.

But she didn't mind that too much. With her engagement ring on her finger and a smile on her face, she was much more interested in spending every moment she could with Rick before he had to go back to base.

Just thinking about living two months without him was depressing. But once that was done, he'd be home to stay and she'd finally have the kind of marriage and family she'd always wanted.

Sarabeth Allen came bustling out of her flower shop when she spotted Sadie through the window. "Sadie, honey," she crooned, leaning in for a hard hug. "How you doing?"

"I'm fine, Sarabeth," she said, a little confused.

"Good for you, honey," Sarabeth said as she gave a passing woman a hard look. "You pay no attention to wagging tongues, you hear me? Some of these old biddies have nothing better to do than spread rumors."

A small twist of worry tugged at the pit of her stomach. "Thanks, Sarabeth. I'll remember."

"See you do," she said, then pulled a hankie from the sleeve of her shirt and wiped her eyes as she looked down at the smiling twins. She muttered, "Poor little mites," just before turning and heading back into her shop.

"What in the world?" Sadie shook her head and continued to the diner. She pushed open the front door and stepped into the blissful cool. She was already late for lunch with Abby. The hazards of having to get *three* people ready before going anywhere.

The women at the booth closest to her dropped their gazes and lowered their voices. That twist of worry tugged a little sharper. But Sadie was determined to not let anything spoil her happiness.

She felt everyone watching her as she walked down the narrow aisle between the red leather booths and the spinning stools at the counter.

"Poor thing," someone whispered a little too loudly.

"He's a no-account," another voice added. "Just like her last man."

Sadie's stomach started spinning.

"Those poor children…"

In the stroller, Wendy and Gail were babbling to each other and slapping their toys against the stroller tray.

"Tsk. Tsk. Tsk. Such pretty girls, too…"

A little irritated as well as worried, Sadie slid onto the bench seat opposite her friend with relief. She threw a wary glance back over her shoulder, then leaned forward and asked, "What's going on, Abby? What's everyone talking about?"

Abby scowled at the people in the diner and shook her head. "Sweetie, it's just the Royal gossips picking up a juicy tidbit to chew on."

"About me?" she asked, handing a soda cracker each to the twins to keep them happy.

"In a roundabout way," Abby said on a sigh. "Sadie, it's all over town, so you have to know. Someone claims to have seen Rick in Midland a couple days before the dance. Having what looked like a cozy lunch with a beautiful brunette."

Sadie felt a hard punch to the center of her chest. She

couldn't speak. Couldn't think. "No. I don't believe it," she said, shaking her head.

Abby sighed heavily. "I wouldn't, either. Rick just doesn't strike me as the cheating kind."

But then, Sadie told herself grimly, her ex-husband hadn't seemed like a cheater either and turned out, he was the cheat to end all cheats. Worry bounced around in the pit of her stomach like a crazed ping-pong ball.

Had she pushed Rick into this marriage? Was he only claiming to love her to get her to agree to marry him? She bit into her bottom lip and chewed at it as nerves rattled through her system.

"Sadie…"

She shook her head. "I've got to go, Abby. I need to think."

"Honey, don't do anything drastic."

Like give Rick back his ring before she made another horrific mistake?

She glanced at the diamond sparkling on her hand and felt the bottom drop out of her world. She didn't want to believe the gossips. Didn't want to think that what was between her and Rick was nothing but smoke and mirrors.

But could she afford to take the risk?

Twelve

It wasn't a risk.

It was a nightmare.

Sadie hadn't wanted to believe the gossips. Hadn't wanted to pay any attention at all to the rumors flying around town. But the pity-filled looks and the whispers she'd faced at lunch with Abby had convinced her to face the problem head-on.

She wasn't the same woman she had been when Taylor Hawthorne had made her a laughingstock. She was strong enough now to face Rick with what she'd heard. To ask him for an explanation.

Which was why she was here now, feeling her heart shatter in her chest.

Sadie's car was parked on the road outside Rick's ranch. She kept the engine running. She wouldn't be staying.

Behind her, in their car seats, the girls shouted, "Daddy! Want Daddy!"

Every word peeled another little slice of her heart away. She swallowed back the urge to cry, blinked to clear her blurred vision and focused on the view of her fiancé standing in the front yard of his ranch house, arguing with a beautiful brunette. Though the ranch was set far back from the road, there was a wide view of the house and, sadly, Sadie had a front-row seat.

"You wanted proof," Sadie told herself sadly.

Even in her stunned shock, even through the pain, Sadie could admit that whoever the woman was, she and Rick looked good together. They looked very *familiar* with each other, too.

When Rick reached out to grab the woman's shoulders, Sadie hissed in a small, wounded breath. Seeing his hands on another woman was just another tiny stab of an emotional blade. The brunette shook her head at him. She looked furious. Well, Sadie thought, she should join the club.

Rick started talking again and whatever he said must have gotten through to the woman because she nodded and smiled just before throwing her arms around Rick's neck and plastering herself against him for a long hug.

The worst part…Rick hugged her back.

"Oh, God." Sadie swiped away a tear rolling down her cheek.

"Daddy!" Gail shouted. "Want Daddy!"

"Wenne, too!" Wendy cried.

Sadie hardly heard the plaintive cries. She was too busy trying to smother her own as she watched the man she loved hugging another woman in his front yard.

The Royal rumor mill had been right, she thought dismally.

He wasn't even hiding his woman away, the bastard. He was right out in the open. Obviously, he didn't care if Sadie found out about her.

"Just like Taylor," she whispered.

She looked down at the diamond sparkling on her finger. Sunlight caught the facets and dazzled her eyes. For three lovely days, she had been happy. Secure in the knowledge that Rick *did* love her. *Did* want a future with her for all of the right reasons. Turned out, though, that he was simply a better actor than she might have given him credit for.

A pretty ring and promises obviously didn't mean a damn thing if she couldn't trust him.

And clearly, she couldn't.

Anger mixed with hurt churned in her stomach and roiled into a toxic stew. If she hadn't had her daughters with her, Sadie would have confronted him. She'd have walked right up to him and his bimbo and told them both exactly what she thought of them. But she wouldn't do that to her babies. No point in scarring them at this tender age. They would find out in time on their own that their father was no good. She wouldn't have to tell them.

"Sorry, babies," she said aloud, throwing the car into gear again with one last look at the man she loved. Thankfully, he hadn't taken his eyes off the brunette long enough to notice her car idling on the road in front of his place. "We're not going to Daddy's house. We're going to take a trip, okay?"

"Want Daddy," Gail whined, kicking her feet against the car seat.

"No go way!" Wendy wailed.

Shaking her head, Sadie winced as a shaft of light danced off her ring and speared into her eyes. Deliberately, she tore the diamond from her hand and tossed it onto the passenger seat beside her. Without the love and promise it represented, that ring was nothing more than a shiny rock.

Pain wrapped itself around her, but she didn't cry. Her eyes burned, but remained dry. There was an emptiness inside her that felt as wide as the sea. She'd found herself. Found her own confidence and now, even that had been shaken. She'd believed in Rick. Trusted him. Allowed herself to love him completely, and losing all of that now was more painful than anything else she had ever known.

Clutching tight to whatever strength she had left, she drove off without a backward glance—so she didn't see Rick look up at the sound of the engine.

She didn't hear him calling after her, either—and wouldn't have cared if she had.

Two hours later, Rick was at the Price mansion, waiting for *someone* to open the damn door. He glanced around, saw cars in the driveway—though not Sadie's. He was hoping she had parked in the garage, but something inside him had fisted into a knot so tight he was choking on it.

So far, this day had gone from bad to worse. And the bad feeling he had lodged in his chest told him it wasn't going to get any better real soon.

"Damn it, Sadie," he shouted, "open the door!"

Still nothing and the silence was starting to freeze him out in spite of the West-Texas sun blasting down on him from a merciless sky.

He'd tried to call Sadie a dozen times since he'd seen her driving away from the ranch. Rick had known immediately what she must be thinking and he'd wanted nothing more than to kick his own ass for hurting her.

He knew damn well what she must be thinking. Hell, what she'd seen, from her point of view, had probably looked bad. She'd seen him with another woman—hugging another woman—and taking into consideration the fact that her last husband was a cheating no-good snake, Rick knew she was probably now convinced that he was no better.

Well, there was a perfectly reasonable explanation for all of this—which he could prove to her if she'd open the damned door and hear him out.

Rick walked down the four steps to the lawn, looked up at the house and glared at the room he knew was hers. "Sadie, come on!"

His shout went unanswered too.

Gritting his teeth in frustration, he raced back up the steps and slammed his knuckles against the heavy wood door. He'd been doing that off and on now for fifteen minutes with no results. So this time, he pounded on the damn thing in a staccato beat that continued until the door was finally jerked open.

Sadie's brother blocked the doorway. His features were tight and hard and he looked about as welcoming as a rattler eyeing its dinner. "Stop beating the door down."

"Where's Sadie?"

"Why should I tell you?"

"You don't want to get in my way on this," Rick warned.

"Funny," Brad mused. "Seems like a good idea to me."

Fury fisted in his guts. Rick pushed his way past

Sadie's brother and stormed into the Price mansion. His boot heels clacked on the flooring as he walked to the bottom of the staircase and shouted, "Sadie!"

"She's not here."

Rick spun around to face his woman's father. The older man looked cold and dispassionate. Just what he would have expected from a man who would have his only daughter sacrifice her own happiness for the family coffers.

For a long, tension-filled minute, the two men stared at each other. Brad was still standing to Rick's left and the animosity coming off him was thick enough to slice. But Rick's focus was on the older man. "Tell me where she is, Mr. Price."

Even relaxing at home, Robert Price wore an elegantly tailored, three-piece suit. He was an imposing man, but Rick wouldn't have cared if the old boy had been holding a loaded shotgun on him. Nothing was going to stop him from finding and talking to Sadie.

The older man turned his back and walked into the formal living room and Rick was just a step or two behind him. Sunlight washed the room in a bright, golden light. But all Rick noticed was the missing baby monitor that Sadie had kept on a side table by her favorite reading chair.

Ice skimmed over his heart.

"My daughter left here not an hour ago," Robert said, settling into a wing-backed chair that, with the old man sitting in it, resembled a throne. "She specifically said that she didn't want to see you."

Rick pulled in a deep breath and fought to keep from raging at the man. "She's going to anyway."

"Why're you here?" Brad interrupted from behind him and Rick threw him an angry glare.

"That's between me and Sadie," he ground out.

"Not anymore," Brad told him flatly. "The whole town's talking about you and your new girlfriend."

"Ah, God…" Misery pumped through him at a staggering pace.

"That's right," Brad told him. Shaking his head he got closer, his gaze sweeping over Rick dismissively. "Did you really think nobody would know? Hell, you grew up here. You know as well as anyone what the gossips in Royal are like."

"Gossip doesn't mean truth," Rick muttered, his gaze locked now with Brad's. Sadie's brother looked as furious as Rick was. The temperature in this brightly sunny room was close to freezing with the two Price men glowering at him.

And damned if Rick could blame either one of them.

"Close enough," Brad maintained. "Plus, Sadie went to see you, to have you explain, and she got an eyeful of you hugging the other woman."

He knew she'd seen that. Which was why he was here. To explain. To make her see that what she was thinking was all wrong.

"She didn't see what she thought she did," he muttered.

"Right!" Brad laughed and looked past Rick to his father. "Hear that, Dad? Sadie's blind now."

"I heard," Robert said softly.

Rick didn't even glance at the older man. Brad was the one he'd deal with. Rubbing one hand across the back of his neck, he said tightly, "Just tell me where she is, and I can take care of this mess. Five minutes with her, that's all I ask."

"Ask all you want. She doesn't owe you anything anymore." Brad dug one hand into his pocket, pulled something free, then flipped it to Rick.

It hit his palm and the instant his fingers closed over it, something in Rick snapped.

Sadie's engagement ring.

Breath straining in his lungs, heartbeat pounding erratically in his chest, he spoke through tightly gritted teeth. "Tell me where she is, Brad."

"You think I'm gonna stand by and watch while my sister's heart gets kicked around the county again? I don't think so. She's lived through the pity of this town once. Why should I help you put her through that again?"

"I *love* her," Rick managed to say.

"Bull." Brad reared back and threw a punch to Rick's jaw that sent him sprawling onto the floor.

Ears ringing, jaw throbbing, Rick scrambled back up, and threw a punch of his own to Brad's gut. Brad staggered and bent over, wheezing for air.

"I figure as her brother, you were owed one shot at me. But you take another one and I'll put you down. Understand?"

"Try it," Brad said, bracing for a fight.

"That's enough." Robert Price stood up and walked to stand in between the two men. He gave his son a quelling look, then turned his gaze on Rick. "Is it true? Do you love my daughter?"

Rick flashed a furious look at Brad before shifting his gaze to meet the older man's. Rubbing one hand over his sore jaw, he muttered, "Yes. I love her. But it's not easy. The Price family's a hardheaded bunch."

Brad snorted. "It's not this family. It's the women in this town."

Robert, though, simply took a minute or two to study Rick in silence. With their eyes locked, it was as if the older man was trying to see into Rick's heart. And at last, he was satisfied.

"I'll tell you where she went—"

"Dad!"

"But if I'm wrong about you," Robert said tellingly, "I'll turn my son loose on you again."

"You're not wrong," Rick said plainly. "I love her. I love my girls. I'll explain everything to you later, but I owe that explanation to Sadie first."

"Agreed," Robert said. "She and the girls are at the Hilton Plaza in Midland."

Rick started for the door instantly. But at the threshold, he turned back. "Just because your boy got one lucky punch in doesn't mean he could take me."

Robert laughed while Brad fumed.

Rick was already gone.

The girls had cried themselves to sleep.

Sadie's soul ached.

And the hotel was out of chocolate ice cream.

"How does that happen in a civilized world?" Sadie asked, making do with room service vanilla topped with chocolate syrup.

Should have gone back to Houston, she thought sadly. As she had the *last* time she'd run from her troubles. But Houston was so much farther away from Royal and home than Midland was. At least here, she could

fool herself into believing that she was still close to…
everybody.

Frowning to herself, she had another bite of ice cream
and let the bland vanilla slide down her throat. Sadie
didn't really like admitting that she had run away. Again.
But how could she have stayed in town while Rick was
romancing a pretty brunette?

"I bet *she* has chocolate ice cream," Sadie muttered
bitterly.

Just as she apparently had *Rick*. But even as she
thought that, she wondered about it. Would a man who
talked about honor and duty the same way another man
talked about his car or job—just another part of his
life—cheat?

Had Rick really been lying to her all along? Or had
she allowed her own pain and shock to color what she
saw?

"Hard to misinterpret a hug like that one," she muttered, remembering how Rick and the brunette had
looked, as melded together as…the chocolate syrup on
her boring vanilla ice cream.

Sighing, she took a bite, licked the spoon, then lifted
one hand to wipe away a stray tear. She hadn't cried
until she got to the hotel. But once there, she'd really
made up for lost time.

It wasn't easy, hiding her tears from her daughters.
But thankfully, the girls were asleep. Which had given
Sadie plenty of time to cry herself silly while waiting
for ice cream that really wasn't cutting it as far as self-
pity-party food.

Now, not only was she unsatisfied in the chocolate
department…her chest hurt, her eyes ached and her nose
was stuffy. One look in the mirror had told her she was

not one of those women who could cry pretty. No, when she cried, her entire body was involved in the process and made her look as though she'd been dragged upside down through hell, feet first.

She used the edge of her spoon to scrape the chocolate syrup off the ice cream. Once it was gone, she sighed unhappily and wondered just how long it would take room service to bring the chocolate cake she had ordered.

The Governor's suite in the Midland Plaza was comfortable, but too darn big for one lonely woman and her twin baby girls. Outside the window, a storm was rolling in, black clouds gathering on the horizon, wind whipping the trees that lined the small lake in front of the hotel. Lightning shimmered in the darkness and the first splats of rain hit the window just as the doorbell of the suite rang.

She hoped the waiter had brought *both* pieces of chocolate cake, Sadie thought. She was going to need them.

Sniffling, she walked to the door, looked through the peephole and gasped when she saw Rick, staring right back at her from the hall. She moved back from the door, shaking her head. She didn't want to see him. Not now. Maybe not ever.

Oh, God. She looked *hideous*.

"Open the door, Sadie."

"No."

"If you don't, I'll make such a big scene out here, people will be talking about it for years."

"That threat would have worked on me once," she said through the door and realized she meant it. She didn't care what anyone thought anymore. She hadn't run away this time because she didn't want to hear gossip.

She'd taken off because she had been too hurt to face Rick.

Okay, yes, she didn't like the pity-filled glances from the gossips in Royal. But the only thing that could *really* hurt her was Rick's betrayal.

"Do you really think I care what anyone in this hotel thinks of me? Or you?" she countered, peering at him through that peephole again. "I don't. And trust me when I say I've seen enough of you today."

She actually heard him sigh. A second later, she was looking through the peephole again, staring into his brown eyes.

"Sadie, what you saw at the ranch—"

Pain slapped at her and her tears dried up. She *really* wanted that chocolate cake. "I already know what I saw. I don't want a recap."

"It wasn't what you think."

"Oh," she said, still watching him, "so she was a stranger and she tripped and you had to catch her in a full-body hug? That must have been terrible for you. *Poor* man."

His jaw worked as if he were biting back a torrent of words. Finally he blew out a frustrated breath, looked directly into the security hole and said, "Fine. You want me to do this in the hallway, I'll do it here."

"I don't want anything from you," she countered hotly. "Except for you to go away."

"Not happening. Not until you hear me out."

"Fine, talk."

He started to, then closed his mouth in irritation before snapping it shut.

"Are you really too big a coward to face me without a door in between us?"

"I'm not a coward. I just don't want you near me."

"So not a coward, just a liar."

Okay, she was lying. She *did* want him. But she wasn't going to share him with a host of women. So she'd just have to learn to do without what she wanted. "Do I have to call security?"

"Sadie," he said on a long sigh, "the woman you saw me with was *Lisa.*"

She laughed harshly, then lowered her voice as she heard the girls start to stir in the adjoining bedroom. "You think I care what her name is?"

"She's the widow of my friend, Jeff. The man who saved my life."

Rick waited for what felt like an eternity. But it was only moments before he heard the security chain slide free, the locks turn. Then the door was open and Sadie was standing there, looking at him.

Her blue eyes were rimmed in red and glassy with the sheen of tears. She had a blot of chocolate syrup at one corner of her mouth and her blond hair was pulled into a crooked ponytail.

She looked unbelievably young and vulnerable and his heart melted in his chest. He loved her more with every breath and if he lived to be a hundred, he still would go to his death complaining that he hadn't had enough time with her.

"My God, you're beautiful," he said softly.

She flushed. "Yes, because splotchy girls are all the rage this season," she sputtered.

"Splotchy girls are my weakness."

She hitched an unsteady breath, backed up so he could enter the suite. "Come in."

He took a quick look around as he walked into the room. It was big, with cream-colored walls, stone-gray carpet and a view of the city. There was a blue velvet couch, a couple of tapestry easy chairs and an open door led to what was probably the girls' bedroom.

He heard her close the door quietly before he turned to look at her. Tossing his hat onto the nearby couch, Rick just looked his fill of her. He'd been so worried that he'd lost her. So shaken, thinking about living a life without her, that he hardly knew what to do now that she was standing in front of him again.

"Jeff's widow?" she asked, and her voice was so soft, he almost didn't catch the words.

"Yeah." He didn't go to her. Not yet. He wanted the air clear between them first. They'd been through so much in the last few weeks. Coming together, finding their way and now, he had to make her see that what they had found was real. That she could trust it. And him.

"Lisa and Jeff actually lived in Houston." He laughed a little. "Funny, two Texas boys meeting in the middle of a war zone on the other side of the planet, but—" he broke off. "That doesn't matter now. The point is, I've met with her a couple of times since I've been back."

"Why didn't you tell me?"

"I should have," he admitted. But Jeff was still an open wound in Rick's heart and soul. Talking about him, even with Sadie, wasn't easy. "It's…hard for me to talk about it."

She scrubbed her hands up and down her arms as if she were cold to the bone. "Okay, I can understand that. But tell me. Why was she at the ranch today?"

"Actually, she drove down to Royal to read me the riot act," he admitted and gave her a rueful smile. "In that, the two of you would probably get along great."

Sadie gave him a sad smile in return, but she didn't say anything. She was still waiting for that explanation.

"Lisa was studying medicine," he said on a long, expelled breath. "But she dropped out of school when she and Jeff got married. They couldn't afford it. She came to the ranch today to yell at me because she just found out that I arranged for her to go back to school. I had my lawyers set up a fund for her books and tuition and anything else she needs."

She took a quick breath, then bit down on her bottom lip as fresh tears pooled in her eyes. Immediately, Rick started talking again.

"It's not because I'm having an affair with her or anything," he insisted. "I'm not in love with her, Sadie. I love you and I would never cheat on you with *anybody.* And, damn it, you should know that about me already."

"Rick…"

Her tone gave away none of what she was feeling, so Rick spoke fast, hoping to make her understand.

"I'm sending her to school because it's what Jeff would have done if he'd come home. He used to talk to me about it. How important it was for him that she find her dreams." He ran one hand over his face and shook his head. "Jeff was so damn proud of her, he wanted to make sure she became a great doctor. Well, he didn't come home. Because of me."

"Rick, no," she said. "It was Jeff's choice to sacrifice himself. You shouldn't second-guess him."

"Can't help it," he admitted. "I'll have that guilt riding me for the rest of my life, Sadie. I'll always know that whatever life I have, whatever *love* I have, Jeff bought it for me. He lost everything so I could come home. I owed it to him to make sure Jeff's dreams for Lisa came true."

"Rick, that is the—"

"I wouldn't cheat on you, Sadie," he told her again quickly, interrupting her because he suddenly needed to say everything he was feeling. "I *love* you. I think I've loved you from the time we were kids. Maybe from that day the waitress spilled a soda in your lap."

Tears were streaking her already puffy face in a steady stream now. But she was smiling and that gave Rick the encouragement he needed. He was in front of her in three long strides.

Pulling her up close to him, he wrapped his arms around her, tucked her head beneath his chin. "I've loved you all my life, Sadie Price. And I will go on loving you until we're old and crabby with great-grandbabies crawling all over us."

She laughed and cried a little harder. But her arms snaked around his waist and held him tightly.

"You should have told me, Rick." Tipping her head back, she stared up at him, heart in her eyes. "Why didn't you?"

He shrugged a little uneasily. "Embarrassed, I guess. Or maybe, I don't know. Maybe I thought you wouldn't understand how much I needed to do this."

"How could I not understand? I say a prayer for Jeff every night, thanking him for bringing you home to me."

"Sadie…"

She reached up, cupping his face between her palms. "Why would you be embarrassed to do the right thing for your friend and his wife?"

Rick smirked a little. "Should have told you. With your help it might not have taken so long to convince Lisa to take the damn money."

"So much pride," she whispered with a slow shake of her head. "So much honor. You're an amazing man, Rick Pruitt."

"If you think so, I'm happy." He bent to kiss her hard, fast. The vise around his heart had eased up a little, making breathing easier, but until she agreed to come back to Royal and marry him, he was a man on the edge. "Come home with me, Sadie. Build a family with me. Let's give the twins six or seven brothers and sisters."

"What?" She laughed, astonished. "Are you crazy?"

"Okay, I'll compromise. Four more kids."

"Three."

"It's negotiable."

"Rick—"

"Marry me, Sadie. Whatever it is you want to do, I'll back your play. Go to school. Get that design degree," he urged. "Hell, be Abby's campaign manager against your brother! I'll help."

She laughed again and the sound was like music to him. It was a balm to his soul and a soothing caress to his heart. He'd never be able to hear it enough.

"I'm done with the Corps, Sadie," he added. "I've done my duty and now it's time for me to be with the family I love. With the woman who makes everything in my life absolutely right."

"Are you sure?" she asked. "I don't want you to one day regret leaving the Corps for me."

"I'm not just doing it for you, darlin'. I need this. I need to be with you."

A single tear slid down her cheek. Shaking her head,

she said, "I love you so much it almost scares me, Rick. When I saw you and Lisa together, I felt my heart break—"

"I'm so sorry—"

"No, it's okay." Smiling up at him, she said, "It's my own fault for taking off instead of just *talking* to you. I should have trusted you. Should have trusted *us*. I promise you, from now on, I will."

"From now on? That sounds promising."

"Daddy!" Two voices, one word.

Rick and Sadie turned as one to watch their daughters toddle into the room. Their hair was tousled from sleep and their little faces were bright with delighted smiles.

"So many beautiful women in my life," Rick said, bending down to sweep both girls up in his arms. Then the three of them faced Sadie.

Heart in her eyes, she smiled, went up on her toes to kiss him again and said, "All I want is to be with you and our kids, Rick. I want us to build the kind of family and home that will shine with the love we make together."

He handed Wendy to her, then dug in his pocket for the ring Brad had tossed to him. Holding it up so the light in the room danced off the diamond, he looked at her. "Then I'm guessing you'll want this back?"

Her lips tugged into a smile. "You saw Brad. Does that explain the bruise on your jaw?"

"It does," he said, "but your brother's got a fist-size ache in his belly, so I figure we're even."

"You hit him?"

"He wouldn't tell me where you were. And, he did hit me first."

"Oh, well, then…"

"Can we not talk about Brad right now?" he asked,

grinning as he waved the ring in front of her face again. "Sadie, just tell me straight up. Am I about to be a married man?"

"You bet you are, Marine," she said, holding up her hand so he could slide the ring onto her finger where it belonged.

"Thank God," he whispered, dipping his head to kiss her again.

The twins clapped their tiny hands and that round of applause was the sweetest sound Rick had ever heard.

He was still kissing her when Wendy shouted, "Go castle!"

Gail patted Rick's cheek and solemnly said, "Castle, Daddy. Home."

Rick's gaze met Sadie's. She smiled up at him and said, "You heard your daughters, Rick. It's time to go *home*."

"Darlin'," he whispered huskily, "nothing in my life has ever sounded better."

* * * * *

*The showdown over the Texas Cattleman's Club
and its future continues in
THE REBEL TYCOON RETURNS
by Katherine Garbera.
Available soon from Harlequin Desire.*

COMING NEXT MONTH

Available August 9, 2011

REQUEST YOUR FREE BOOKS!

2 FREE NOVELS PLUS 2 FREE GIFTS!

Harlequin® *Desire*

ALWAYS POWERFUL, PASSIONATE AND PROVOCATIVE

YES! Please send me 2 FREE Harlequin Desire® novels and my 2 FREE gifts (gifts are worth about $10). After receiving them, if I don't wish to receive any more books, I can return the shipping statement marked "cancel." If I don't cancel, I will receive 6 brand-new novels every month and be billed just $4.30 per book in the U.S. or $4.99 per book in Canada. That's a saving of at least 14% off the cover price! It's quite a bargain! Shipping and handling is just 50¢ per book in the U.S. and 75¢ per book in Canada.* I understand that accepting the 2 free books and gifts places me under no obligation to buy anything. I can always return a shipment and cancel at any time. Even if I never buy another book, the two free books and gifts are mine to keep forever.

225/326 HDN FEF3

Name	(PLEASE PRINT)
Address	Apt. #
City	State/Prov.	Zip/Postal Code

Signature (if under 18; a parent or guardian must sign)

Mail to the **Reader Service**:
IN U.S.A.: P.O. Box 1867, Buffalo, NY 14240-1867
IN CANADA: P.O. Box 609, Fort Erie, Ontario L2A 5X3

Not valid for current subscribers to Harlequin Desire books.

Want to try two free books from another line?
Call 1-800-873-8635 or visit www.ReaderService.com.

* Terms and prices subject to change without notice. Prices do not include applicable taxes. Sales tax applicable in N.Y. Canadian residents will be charged applicable taxes. Offer not valid in Quebec. This offer is limited to one order per household. All orders subject to credit approval. Credit or debit balances in a customer's account(s) may be offset by any other outstanding balance owed by or to the customer. Please allow 4 to 6 weeks for delivery. Offer available while quantities last.

Your Privacy—The Reader Service is committed to protecting your privacy. Our Privacy Policy is available online at www.ReaderService.com or upon request from the Reader Service.

We make a portion of our mailing list available to reputable third parties that offer products we believe may interest you. If you prefer that we not exchange your name with third parties, or if you wish to clarify or modify your communication preferences, please visit us at www.ReaderService.com/consumerschoice or write to us at Reader Service Preference Service, P.O. Box 9062, Buffalo, NY 14269. Include your complete name and address.

*Once bitten, twice shy. That's Gabby Wade's motto—
especially when it comes to Adamson men.
And the moment she meets Jon Adamson her theory
is confirmed. But with each encounter a little something
sparks between them, making her wonder if she's been
too hasty to dismiss this one!*

*Enjoy this sneak peek from ONE GOOD REASON
by Sarah Mayberry, available August 2011
from Harlequin® Superromance®.*

Gabby Wade's heartbeat thumped in her ears as she marched to her office. She wanted to pretend it was because of her brisk pace returning from the file room, but she wasn't that good a liar.

Her heart was beating like a tom-tom because Jon Adamson had touched her. In a very male, very possessive way. She could still feel the heat of his big hand burning through the seat of her khakis as he'd steadied her on the ladder.

It had taken every ounce of self-control to tell him to unhand her. What she'd really wanted was to grab him by his shirt and, well, explore all those urges his touch had instantly brought to life.

While she might not like him, she was wise enough to understand that it wasn't always about liking the other person. Sometimes it was about pure animal attraction.

Refusing to think about it, she turned to work. When she'd typed in the wrong figures three times, Gabby admitted she was too tired and too distracted. Time to call it a day.

As she was leaving, she spied Jon at his workbench in the shop. His head was propped on his hand as he studied blueprints. It wasn't until she got closer that she saw his eyes were shut.

He looked oddly boyish. There was something innocent and unguarded in his expression. She felt a weakening in her resistance to him.

"Jon." She put her hand on his shoulder, intending to shake him awake. Instead, it rested there like a caress.

His eyes snapped open.

"You were asleep."

"No, I was, uh, visualizing something on this design." He gestured to the blueprint in front of him then rubbed his eyes.

That gesture dealt a bigger blow to her resistance. She realized it wasn't only animal attraction pulling them together. She took a step backward as if to get away from the knowledge.

She cleared her throat. "I'm heading off now."

He gave her a smile, and she could see his exhaustion.

"Yeah, I should, too." He stood and stretched. The hem of his T-shirt rose as he arched his back and she caught a flash of hard male belly. She looked away, but it was too late. Her mind had committed the image to permanent memory.

And suddenly she knew, for good or bad, she'd never look at Jon the same way again.

Find out what happens next in ONE GOOD REASON,
available August 2011 from Harlequin® Superromance®!

Celebrating

Blaze

10 years of

red-hot reads

Featuring a special August author lineup of
six fan-favorite authors who have written
for Blaze™ from the beginning!

The Original Sexy Six:

Vicki Lewis Thompson
Tori Carrington
Kimberly Raye
Debbi Rawlins
Julie Leto
Jo Leigh

Pick up all six Blaze™
Special Collectors' Edition titles!

August 2011

Plus visit
HarlequinInsideRomance.com
and click on the Series Excitement Tab
for exclusive Blaze™ 10th Anniversary content!

www.Harlequin.com

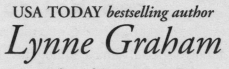

USA TODAY *bestselling author*
Lynne Graham
introduces her new Epic Duet

THE VOLAKIS VOW
A marriage made of secrets…

Tally Spencer, an ordinary girl with no experience of relationships… Sander Volakis, an impossibly rich and handsome Greek entrepreneur. Sander is expecting to love her and leave her, but for Tally this is love at first sight. Little does he know that Tally is expecting his baby…and blackmailing him to marry her!

PART ONE:
THE MARRIAGE BETRAYAL
Available August 2011

PART TWO:
BRIDE FOR REAL
Available September 2011

Available only from Harlequin Presents®.